GOT MEN?

G.A. HAUSER

GOT MEN?

Cover photographer Josh Williams
Cover model Chris Salvatore
Edited by Stacey Rhodes
Cover art by Stephanie Vaughan
ISBN Trade paperback: 978-1450-5520-3-5
The G.A. Hauser Collection

WARNING

This book contains material that maybe offensive to some: graphic language, homosexual relations, adult situations. Please store your books carefully where they cannot be accessed by underage readers.

First G.A. Hauser publication: April 2010

ABOUT THE COVER MODEL

Chris Salvatore started his career in entertainment as a singer/songwriter, writing his first song at age 15. After graduating high school he studied vocal performance at one of America's finest music institutions, Berklee College of Music in Boston, Massachusetts. Chris started gaining notable attention with the release of his debut album *After All Is Said And Done.* His song *Done To Me* was recently featured on MTV's Paris Hilton's My New BFF. In 2006 Chris decided to move to New York City to attend The New York Conservatory for Dramatic Arts and study acting. It was there where he discovered his passion for film and theater. He moved to Los Angeles in 2009 and 2 weeks later was cast in his first feature film as one of the lead roles in *Eating Out: All You Can Eat*. He continues to write music, and even has one of his songs featured on the *Eating Out: All You Can Eat* soundtrack. Chris plans on releasing his 2nd album in 2010.

www.chris-salvatore.com

Josh Williams Photography
941.306.8263
www.joshwilliamsphotography.com

Chapter One

Conrad Hogan had no clue what to pack. Though the idea of participating in a reality TV show excited him, he was slightly unsettled by the lack of information from the show's producers, Derek Dixon and Will Markham. How could he go wrong signing on with the team that created *Forever Young*? That late- night cable television series was number one for its first two seasons and everyone expected it to keep running for a dozen more.

Got Men? Got Men? What the hell kind of name is that?

His apartment buzzer sounded. Conrad jumped out of his skin. He pushed the talk button, "Yeah?" then the listen button.

"Conrad Hogan?"

"Yes?"

"I'm from the reality television show, *Got Men?* I'm here to take you to the house."

Shit. Shit. "Okay. Be right down." Conrad checked his watch and knew he had no choice now but to just go for it. Some people ended up celebrities after being on these shows. He hoped he was one of them. At least that or it would get him a job. Being unemployed sucked.

After only one interview with Will and Derek, Conrad signed the contract. He didn't even read it. There was so much fine print on the thing, he doubted he'd understand it.

Taking a last look around his sparsely furnished studio apartment in Elk Grove, California, Conrad shouldered his backpack, carried his suitcase and shut off the lights. He walked down the two flights of stairs and noticed a man in a suit waiting outside the door.

The minute the man noticed him, he reached for his large bag and walked to a limousine parked out in front of his building.

Conrad looked back at his abode as he handed the man his rucksack, wondering if the next time he saw it, he'd be a changed man.

Sitting in the back seat, Conrad comfortably straddled his legs and tried to make idle conversation. The driver didn't even share his first name with him. After being ignored or given grunts and one word answers, Conrad shut up.

He wasn't even told where he was going to live while participating in the event. It wasn't like Big Brother. No one was expected to be evicted. It was just a test of endurance and sanity. That was all Conrad got out of the show's description. A few guys with the bare essentials trying to last. No voting off, no embarrassing parting tears, no vying for a rich person's hand in marriage, nothing like that.

Just a few people cohabitating.

I may be only twenty-three, but I know these types of shows better than that. Something's going to happen. They just won't tell us what.

Conrad recalled the list of information he been required to reveal on written forms, before he was offered a spot on the show. He was asked about his health, physically and mentally, and even given a check-up by their doctor. One question he'd had to answer bothered Conrad and he almost left it blank.

Sexual orientation.

Was that anyone's business? What did it matter?

He had skipped it until Will Markham pointed it out. Will

slid the paper back to Conrad and waited. Conrad reluctantly checked one box and slid it back.

The moment Will had read the answer, he said, “I want you in.”

It was no secret Will Markham was gay. He even showed up to the Emmys with his live-in lover, the photographer Madison Henning.

Conrad tried not to see a connection to his sexual orientation and his acceptance on the show. Was he the ‘token’ gay guy? Opened up to be teased mercilessly by a house full of homophobic jocks?

“Oh, please God, no.” He wrung his hands and tried to figure out where the chauffeur was going. After a couple of hours on Interstate 80, Conrad read a sign welcoming them to Nevada. He knew he was in for one wild ride.

He had no idea if he was arriving last, first or somewhere in between.

The driver escorted him and his luggage up the steps of a two-story home that was completely surrounded by a fourteen foot wooden fence. The area was barren surrounding the island-like home and there were no neighbors for miles. Conrad assumed the house was constructed for this event. He even spotted debris from the site still sitting in a vacant lot along with a port-o-potty across the dirt road.

Though the residence was enormous and glitzy looking, on close inspection Conrad could read the signs of pre-fabrication and imitation veneer. He’d been in construction long enough to see through the junk they used to build new homes. It was beginning to look like a studio set. A fake backdrop.

He stopped in the foyer.

“Welcome to *Got Men?*, Conrad.”

Conrad reached out his hand. “You’re Charlotte Deavers.”

“I am. I’ll be the host of the show.”

"Yes. I remember Will Markham mentioning that. I love *Forever Young*."

"Flattery will get you nowhere." Charlotte grinned at him. "Come this way. I'll show you to your room." When he headed up the stairs, which gave him a chance to walk completely through the bottom floor to the back of the house, Conrad spotted an open-planned kitchen with an island topped with white marble, and a large dining room table. Across from the kitchen was a lounge/living area with several overstuffed sectional sofas, a chair and ottoman and a coffee table. Near the back end of the house was a gym, and a room with its door shut. Behind the slatted stairs to the second floor Conrad caught sight of the backyard with a kidney shaped in-ground pool and hot tub. He admired the limited view of the fenced in patio and continued his excursion to the upper floor. It consisted of a long hallway with six doors facing it.

"This bedroom is yours." Charlotte opened the first door to the right.

Conrad stepped in. The driver had his entire bag's contents strewn on the bed. "What the fuck?"

"He's just checking for electronics."

"Jesus. He could have asked."

"You're next." Charlotte's grin was unnerving him.

"Next to do what? Search a bag?"

"No. Get searched."

As she said those words, the driver, who appeared pinched, began turning Conrad's pockets inside out. In reaction, Conrad held up his hands as if he was being robbed. "Why don't you ask? I would have done it for you."

"Rules." Charlotte bit at a hangnail. "You read the contract, right?"

"Sure," he lied.

His wallet and keys were thrown onto the bed with his belongings. The man muttered to Charlotte, "He's good," and left.

"Good boy." Charlotte smiled. "I love it when I'm obeyed." She checked her watch. "Okay. This space is all yours. That thing on the dresser is a microphone. You have to have it on every minute you're here. This thing," She picked up a small video camera, "Is for your personal thoughts. Before bed, whatever, it's a live feed to the net, and if you say anything juicy it'll be aired on television." She held it up to him. "Just press this record button and point it at your face. Some people hold it, others set it on the dresser and sit on the foot of the bed. You'll figure it out." She put it back down.

It was such an overload, he was already lost and stopped paying attention to her. Conrad noticed a camera in the corner of the room pointed at his bed. "Wide angle?"

"Of course. You can't hide, sweetie."

"Uh, do we share a bathroom?"

"Not unless you want to." Her wicked grin was making him so anxious he began to shake. She must know he was gay or something. "That door." She pointed. "Behind that door there's a small closet and that's the bathroom."

Conrad had a look. A camera was in the bathroom as well. "You watch me take a shit?"

"Yeah. Everything. You did read the contract, right?'

He opened the closet. A camera was set up there as well. "Holy cow."

"Okay, sweetums. I have more people to show around. Be in the lounge at five and we'll introduce all the housemates to the world and each other." She threw him a kiss and shut the door.

He was dazed, staring at the pile clothing on his bed. "What the hell did I do this for?"

Chapter Two

Though he did hear voices down the hall, Conrad didn't open the door. He busied himself folding his clothing and hanging up his good shirts and trousers. Setting his toiletries out on the bathroom sink, he tried not to stare into the multitude of camera lenses which watched his every move. The shower was concealed by a frosted curtain; just enough to catch a fleshy burr but not enough to see genitals through it. He imagined hanging all his towels on the shower rod to help hide.

The entire suite smelled new. The paint, the carpet, the bedding, everything was right out of a DIY store or plastic package.

The paddle fan over the bed was spinning, but Conrad opened the window as well. Nevada in March. It was perfect weather. Not a cloud floated in the sky. His view of the pool was outstanding, but he also could see beyond the fence. Nothing but desert and a couple of power poles he assumed were just installed. One enormous satellite dish also loomed, broadcasting to the entire planet.

Conrad picked up the mini-cam and pointed it at himself. He recorded, "I'm insane," and set it back down on the dresser. No phone, no internet, no TV, no radio, no iPod. He checked his watch again. It was nearing five. He had changed into his best outfit while hiding behind his hanging clothing in the closet under the camera's watchful eye. He inspected his reflection quickly in the mirror on the dresser and threw up his hands. He couldn't put it off. He had signed a contract. *Shoulda read it. Fuck.*

Tucking in his shirt into his slacks, clipping on the microphone, Conrad headed down the stairs to the lounge, as he promised Charlotte he would.

A camera crew, consisting of two men, was standing at the entrance.

"Come, Conrad!" Charlotte waved him over jubilantly.

He gave her a slight smile and looked into the lounge. Five men were already there. Conrad gulped audibly when he inspected them. *Holy mother-of-god.*

Charlotte placed her hand on Conrad's shoulder. "Conrad, this is Dean."

He extended his hand to a stunning male probably in his late twenties, with short brown hair and brown eyes, obviously showing off the tattoos which ran down both arms like sleeves. "Hey."

"Hey." Dean shook his hand.

Charlotte nudged Conrad to the next man. "Alfonso, this is Conrad."

In what Conrad assumed was an attempt at keeping some anonymity, none of their last names were used. He salivated at the sight of Alfonso's imposing six-foot two inch height, jet black hair and designer stubble. He was wearing a midriff that showed off a belly button ring and the edge of a tattoo that seemed to run below his waist.

"Next, is Tony. Tony, say hi to Conrad." Charlotte appeared so amused, Conrad wondered if he was the only one not in on some private joke.

He shook Tony's hand and wished his cock would behave. Each man was better looking than the next. This one had olive toned skin and an eagle tattoo on his shoulder, a short well-trimmed goatee and dark wicked eyes. When he greeted

Conrad, Conrad heard a New York accent from Tony instantly. "How ya doin'?"

"Good." Conrad released his hand and swallowed down a dry throat when Charlotte brought him towards a fabulous African American stud.

"This is Sonny."

The size of Sonny's biceps almost made Conrad cream. He admired Sonny's shaved head and diamond earrings before he was riveted to Sonny's gaze. "Hi, Conrad."

"Hi." Conrad was going insane. It was a smorgasbord of gay male fantasies.

"Last but not least," Charlotte said, "Conrad, this is Kelvin."

A young man with a baby-face and blond ponytail extended his hand. "Wassup?"

"Hi." Conrad was so hot from all the man-flesh in the room, he was sure his cheeks were pure red.

"Right." Charlotte backed up and waved over the cameramen. "Let's begin, boys."

Conrad cleared his throat and crossed his hands in front of his crotch to hide his excitement, taking his place to stand between Kelvin and Dean with his back to the wall.

Charlotte gave a grand sweeping wave of the group as she hammed it up for the camera lens. "Ladies and gentlemen, here are our delightful contestants in the latest reality television show, *Got Men?*"

As she rattled off her monologue, Conrad wondered if they were indeed contestants, and what was the contest? No votes? No mystery weddings or dates? What on earth could this be about? Was he the only one in the dark? He couldn't wait to get one of the guys alone to…

Conrad remembered. He had a microphone on. No writing utensils. If he asked any controversial questions, everyone would hear. He wondered if he cared. His curiosity was overtaking his fear.

"And they will be filmed night and day, twenty-four hours, non-stop…"

Conrad had been looking down but when he glanced up he caught a sizzling stare directed his way from Sonny. *Oh-my-God. I've never gone with a black guy and, Christ, I have always wanted to. I'm going to die.*

He forced himself to look away. Alfonso was giving him a good once over.

What the fuck? What the fuck?

Conrad seriously began to panic. It felt like a night out in Soho. *Is this the game? Five straight guys try to seduce me? And if I succumb to their charms I get tossed out? Ridiculed? Exposed?*

I'm not out. I'm not out to my family, my friends. No. I'm not falling for this shit.

"…and we'll assign each housemate tasks every day…but they are on their own as far as being limited to talking only to each other with no outside interference…"

Conrad didn't care what Charlotte was saying any longer. He felt betrayed. *So is this why Will asked if I was gay? And immediately signed me up when he found out I was?*

He glanced at Tony. The man was so intense looking and wild, Conrad had to force his gaze away as Tony inspected him.

"Here they are, introduced to you one by one." Charlotte lowered her microphone. On a small monitor she was viewing, the pre-taped interviews they had filmed with Will Markham and Derek Dixon began to run. Conrad perked up and paid close attention.

Dean appeared shy on screen, averting his deep-set, brown eyes and brushing his hair back from his forehead. "Yeah…uh…I'm a tattoo artist from Phoenix. I don't dislike anything and am really looking forward to this experience."

In his interview, Kelvin puffed up his chest and appeared

cocky. "I want to be an actor. I do some local theater in Seattle. Now? Now I'm just waiting tables, you know, until I get my big break."

Conrad tried to meet Kelvin's eyes to smile, but it seemed all the men had their attention glued to the monitor.

Alfonso said to the interviewer, "I'm from Orange County. I'm a private fitness instructor. I specialize in helping people maintain once they've lost weight. I love my job."

That explains his fabulous abs. Conrad imagined chewing on Alfonso's belly button ring.

"Yeah, uh..." Tony looked like a parody of 'Vinnie Barbarino' from *Welcome Back Kotter*. "I'm a teacher in the Bronx. Love riding my Harley. You know."

Sonny was next. He was so soft-spoken, Conrad stepped closer so he could hear the interview. "I'm still working through my medical degree at the University of Pennsylvania, and I'm also a volunteer firefighter."

I'm going to cream! Agh.

His turn. He gulped and every man glanced at him first before his pre-taped conversation.

"Yes, I'm Conrad...I'm in construction, but out of work now, but I'm always looking to better myself. I live in Elk Grove, California and really love it there."

It felt strange to see his own face on film. It didn't even look like him. It was just some dim-witted, brawny, blond guy from off a building site. He thought he sounded stupid. *Geez, put me on camera after the doctor in training. Don't I look pathetic now?*

Charlotte made a signal to the camera crew. The red record light lit on the camera. "There you have it, ladies and gentleman. Our six men who dared to take this challenge. I'm sure it's going to be an interesting experiment."

Experiment? Do I feel even more like a lab rat than ever?

Conrad realized he was holding his breath from nerves. He

forced himself to exhale.

"Okay, gentlemen. You're on your own for the night. I hope someone can cook because you can't call for a pizza." Charlotte headed to the front door, the cameras following her. "Goodnight! See you tomorrow!" She drew her finger under her chin. "Cut." She addressed the room occupants, "Okay, guys. See you in the morning. You should have everything you need, if not, let me know. Bye." She left, the camera crew trailing behind her.

Conrad could hear the door lock from the outside. He looked around the room. "Anyone cook?"

"We can all pitch in." Sonny left the lounge and crossed the space to the kitchen.

"I want a pizza. Why did she mention pizza?" Tony asked.

"Even without the interview, I could tell from your accent you're a New Yorker," Dean said.

"You're a rocket scientist."

"Hey, no need to be nasty."

"Uh oh." Kelvin shook his head. "We got a live one, fellas."

"Guys," Conrad whispered, "All this is being taped." He tilted his head to the wide angle camera lens in the kitchen.

As Alfonso stuck his head into the refrigerator to investigate, Conrad leaned near Sonny. As quietly as he could he whispered, "What do they do to you if you take off the mike?"

"You get a punishment detail, like you have to clean. I think you get bathroom duty. There was a list of infractions in the contract. Didn't you read it?"

Conrad felt like an idiot. "Not all of it."

Sonny laughed, but it wasn't mocking. It was good natured. So far, Sonny was Conrad's favorite, but he was biased. Med student? Firefighter? And downright gorgeous.

He'd been craving black cock for so long he wondered why he'd never gone for it before.

"Okay, guys," Alfonso announced. "Looks like a healthy diet. Protein, veggies…"

"Right up your alley," Dean said. "Do you do nutrition as well as exercise?"

"Yup." Alfonso began placing items on the counter. "Can any of you dudes make a salad?"

"Sure." Conrad rolled up his sleeves and washed his hands.

"I'll find a bowl and stuff." Kelvin began opening cabinets.

"This is too easy," Dean said. "What's the catch?'

All five men spun around and stared at him. For the first time, Conrad realized he wasn't the only one who was confused by this game.

"Believe me. We'll find out. Nuthin's like it seems." Tony slammed the head of iceberg lettuce on the counter loudly. When everyone gaped at him he said, "What? Opens the leaves up."

"Are you from the Sopranos?" Kelvin laughed. "Which bedroom are you in. I hope it isn't near mine."

"What? Am I supposed to kill you in your sleep? I'm a school teacher, for Christ's sake."

Conrad peeled a carrot over the garbage disposal. "Man, I find that incredible. If I had a kid, you'd scare him to death."

"Nah. They love me."

Sonny asked, "Any of you guys have kids?"

Conrad spun around and checked for a response. "No kids. Okay. That makes sense. Married?" Again, Conrad got negative reactions.

Under his breath, Kelvin asked, "You think if we keep trying to figure this out, we'll get nailed?"

"Why are you whispering?" Sonny grinned. "You've got a mike on."

"Hello!" Alfonso waved at the camera on the wall.

Everyone laughed about it.

"Unreal." Conrad gave Tony the carrot since he was slicing and dicing on a cutting board. "What can I do, Alfonso?"

"There's a load of chicken breasts. I hope you guys like chicken."

A chorus of affirmatives surrounded them.

"Okay. I'll just grill them up." Alfonso said to Conrad, "See if there's a grill under the stove. Anything to make nice crosshatch marks."

Sonny said, "Found the salt and pepper." He placed them on the table.

"You can just throw that salt away." Alfonso pointed to the trash. "Stuff's poison."

"You have to use it to season the meat," Tony said, whacking the cucumber with a large chopping knife as if he meant to dismember it.

"You guys salt your own. I don't use the shit. You know how much salt you need a day? Fifteen hundred milligrams. You know you get eight-hundred in two slices of American cheese? Keep the salt away from me."

"I want salt on my salty pretzels." Tony gave Alfonso a teasing glare. "Salt everything."

"Don't antagonize him." Sonny began setting the dining table.

Conrad was enjoying the banter and could read the personalities already. Though Tony played Mr. Tough-guy, Conrad had a feeling he was a pussy cat. And though Kelvin showed cockiness? Conrad guessed he was the youngest and most insecure. To test his theory he went around the room. "I'm twenty-three. How old are you guys? Come on."

Dean said, "I'm probably the oldest. I'm twenty-seven."

"Beat ya." Tony dumped a handful of sliced cucumber into

the large ceramic bowl he had been using. "Thirty-two. Top that."

I would like to top that. Conrad chided himself for his nasty thoughts.

"I'm the youngest. I already know." Kelvin blushed. "I'm twenty-one."

Sonny laughed. "I'm twenty-five, going on fifty-five."

"Why's that?" Conrad asked, bringing paper napkins to help him set the table.

"I feel that way. Med school is murder."

"Come on, Fonzie," Tony asked Alfonso. "How old?"

Alfonso pointed a warning finger at him. "That nickname better not stick." He glanced around the room. "Twenty-five."

"Dean?" Conrad asked.

"Twenty-seven. Not much of a gap between Kelvin and Tony. Ten years. Think they did that on purpose?"

"Yes. They did everything for a reason." Sonny returned to the island counter and leaned on it. "We just don't know what that reason is yet."

Conrad watched Alfonso sear the chicken in a grill pan. "Anyone want to speculate?"

Dean sat on a stool next to Sonny at the counter. "They said no one gets voted off."

"Right." Conrad nodded. "I think there were no blind dates either. No weird cougar-millionaire-farmer crap."

"What the hell does that leave?" Tony wiped his hands on a towel.

"No clue." Dean sank down so his chin was propped on his palm.

"Look," Sonny said, "We'll find out soon enough. Let's just try and get along and not come to blows over anything."

"Why you lookin' at me?" Tony puffed up and tapped his own chest.

Kelvin cracked up with laughter. “You lookin’ at me?” he did his best Robert De Niro accent.

“Kelvin. What the hell kind of name is that?” Tony placed the salad on the table. “You named after the temperature gauge?”

“Here we go.” Dean shook his head. “Is there booze? Are we allowed booze?”

“Yeah, get Vinnie Barbarino drunk. Great idea,” Conrad scoffed.

“Vinnie Barbarino?” Tony gaped at him. “How old are you?”

“I watched the reruns. What?” Conrad laughed. “Do I look fifty?”

“You called me Fonzie. If you dish it out, take it,” Alfonso said.

“This is dinner?” Kelvin gaped. “Chicken and salad? Seriously?”

“Make your own.” Alfonso began placing the cooked chicken on a platter.

Conrad checked the fridge. “No salad dressing.”

“There’s oil and vinegar.” Alfonso asked, “Can you mix up dressing?”

“Just put the two in a bottle?” Conrad asked.

“Who found the salt and pepper?” Alfonso said.

“Me,” Sonny replied.

“Was there a spice rack?”

“Yes.”

When Sonny moved to go to the cabinet, Conrad stopped him. “I’ll do it.” He opened a door and spun a revolving rack. “What do you recommend?”

“What’s there?”

“You don’t expect me to read them all.”

Alfonso put his hands on his hips and gave Conrad an exasperated look.

A sensation of disorientation washed over Conrad. *That is so gay. What? Alfonso's gay? No. I'm nuts.*

"Get going. I'll do it." Alfonso nudged Conrad over and checked out the selection.

"Did someone say there was or wasn't booze?" Tony stood near the dining room table.

"No booze." Dean sat down near him.

"They didn't say 'no booze' in the rules." Kelvin took a seat.

"What are we supposed to do?" Sonny relaxed on a dining room chair.

"I want booze!" Tony shouted at the camera.

A male voice replied back over an amplifier, making all the men jump out of their skin. "Be good and you'll get some."

"What the fuck?" Conrad doubled over with laughter. "Holy shit!"

His hilarity set off a chain reaction of giggles and chuckling. Alfonso returned to the table, shaking a small cruet. "That's Will Markham. I know that voice." He placed the dressing on the table and sat down. "Hi, William!" he waved at the camera lens.

All six were seated and passing the chicken and vegetables.

"I'll drop weight eating like this." Kelvin frowned. I'm already only one-fifty. I can't lose anymore."

"Does anyone work out?" Conrad asked as he gave the cruet a last shake before he used it.

Everyone said yes.

"I should have figured."

"Why?" Tony chewed his food. "Shoulda figured we're all gym-junkies? What's that mean?"

"Look at us." Conrad thought that was pretty obvious.

"You checking our bodies out, Conny?" Tony grinned.

"Again with the nicknames?" Alfonso shook his head. "Give it a rest, man."

Conrad felt pale. The last thing he needed was to be the butt of gay jokes by someone as sharp and biting as Tony-the-Bronx-Tiger. Focusing on his meal, Conrad chided himself to shut up. He didn't need this kind of crap. At a touch to his leg, he jerked his head up to Sonny, who was sitting beside him. Sonny gave him a look that Conrad interpreted as, 'Ignore him'.

Conrad smiled and wanted to clasp that warm hand. But as soon as it had touched him, it retreated.

Other than small talk, the conversation dried up.

With no entertainment other than each other, Conrad hid in the back of the closet as he changed into a pair of workout shorts and a tank top. He knew the camera could see his back, but he wasn't ready to expose his dick to the World Wide Web yet.

Hearing a few of the guys talking together in the lounge, Conrad entered the gym and tossed a small hand towel down, stretching in front of a wall of mirrors.

"We both had the same idea."

Conrad caught Sonny's reflection in the mirror. Shirtless, the only thing covering Sonny's fantastic figure were a pair of faded white football leggings, cut above the knee. As his cock reacted to the stimulation, Conrad pressed his fingers between his legs in a reflex reaction. "Am I the only guy in here without tats?"

Sonny laughed and reached his hands over his head to stretch his back. "Are you? I haven't noticed."

And I have? They'll all know I'm gay. I am so dead.

"I…I just spotted them on a few of the guys." *Good save, you dipshit.* Conrad began loading up the bar for bench presses.

“Cool.” Kelvin poked his head in. “Mind if I run on the treadmill?”

“Nope.” Sonny pushed a pin into the pulley machine and started working his back and shoulders.

“Must be boredom setting in.” Alfonso, also shirtless, entered the room.

Conrad sat on the bench and snuck a peak at his six-pack abs. he could see the edge of that tattoo with more clarity as it was exposed by his hip-hugging spandex shorts. It was of a stylized tribal heart, just done in black. Tasteful. So tasteful, Conrad wanted to lick it.

His naval piercing was a silver ring and he obviously either shaved or waxed his body, because his jaw was dark with that fabulous designer stubble, yet his body was hairless.

Alfonso stood on the second treadmill next to Kelvin.

“Wow. We’ll be so bored we’ll all be cut like models.” Dean entered the room in a torn t-shirt and sweatpants smattered with gaping holes. A towel was slung around his neck.

“Where’s Mr. T?” Sonny asked as he took a break between his sets.

“You callin’ me?” Tony appeared behind Dean.

Conrad had to stifle his ‘wow’. Tony did not shave his chest and proudly displayed his black curling hair which was perfect: an inverted triangle between his pecs which led to a treasure trail and the top of jet black pubic hair.

Conrad had to look away to not embarrass himself. He was already sporting a stiff one.

“Damn. You beat me to the bench.”

Conrad swallowed down a dry throat. “You can work in.”

“Thanks, Conny.”

“Am I stuck with that the entire time I’m in here with you, *Vinnie*?”

"You think I mind you callin' me Vinnie?" Tony laughed. "I've got a cousin Vinnie."

"Why does that not surprise me?" Conrad hefted the weight off the mounts, holding them over his chest for his set.

"You stereotyping Italians, Conny?"

"Guys?" Sonny moaned. "Come on. I can't take this for three weeks. Cool it."

"It's not me." Tony pressed his hand to his hairy chest. "Tell Conny to stop."

Conrad did a few lifts and put the weight down. "Here. Take it." He sat up.

"Aw, don't get your panties in a bunch. Work in with me."

"No." Conrad stood, heading to the only machine left. A stationary bike. He stared at it, did not find it appealing, and caught sight of the pool. That *was* appealing.

Drawn to the blue and pink lights that illuminated under the water, Conrad left through the back sliding door and admired the area. Umbrellas topped glass tables, lounge chairs were abundant, and an array of toys were on display including beach balls, foam noodles, and flying disks. He stared at the selection and tossed a yellow float into the pool, stripping off his shirt, which had the microphone attached and draped it on a chair. Diving in, he climbed on the raft and relaxed, staring at the stars in the velvety black sky.

Other than Tony, he liked everyone. It seemed for these shows, they usually picked an instigator to torment the rest. He'd watched reality television enough to know Tony was selected for his aggression.

A noise from the door caught his attention. If it was Tony he was going to kill him. It wasn't.

"You okay?"

"It'll take more than a few words from that ass to bother me, Sonny."

Sonny sat down and dipped his legs into the pool, kicking gently. "One asshole out of six. That's pretty good odds."

Conrad used his arms to swim closer, holding the edge of the pool next to Sonny. "I'm glad you're here. I need someone smart to keep me sane."

Sonny smiled, appearing flattered. "What makes you think the other guys aren't smart?"

"Med school? You kidding me? I'm in awe."

"Don't be. I haven't gotten through it yet."

Conrad looked at the house. Through the back window he could see the rest of the group still in the gym, smiling, laughing. He wondered if he was the butt of their jokes.

"You said you were from California?"

"Yes." Conrad gave Sonny his attention.

"I have no idea where Elk Grove is."

"North. Near Sacramento."

"Ah." Sonny nodded. "I was born and raised in Philly. This is my first time in…" Sonny smiled. "Nevada? I assumed we were in Nevada because I spotted a sign for Reno."

"That's my guess. I'm surprised we weren't blindfolded."

Conrad caught Sonny searching the area.

"Yes, there are cameras. There and there." Conrad pointed to them attached to the back of the house.

"And there are microphones everywhere. So don't think by taking yours off you can talk."

"Now, now, Sonny." Conrad smiled, "I have nothing to hide."

Sonny leaned over his knees to speak softly. "They have night-vision cameras. You can't even lie in bed and jack-off without them seeing it."

"Should have read the contract." Conrad wasn't surprised by the information. "What's the goal? Did they say? What's the main point?"

"I don't know. To be honest, I'm not a reality show fan. I spent a few days on the net trying to see what I was in for. This show isn't like any of the others."

"I know. I wish I could figure out what the catch is. There has to be some kind of twist."

Sonny glanced over his shoulders at a camera quickly, then smiled. "It's an experiment in human nature. Like rats in a maze."

Conrad smiled but soon felt intimidated.

After hearing a splash, Sonny stood in the pool next to Conrad, giving him a wicked smirk.

"No!"

"Heh heh." Sonny flipped the raft and dunked Conrad into the water.

When Conrad surfaced Sonny was lying on his float, grinning mischievously at him. Conrad stood behind the pillow and motored Sonny around the pool, bumping him into the sides, making him laugh.

Their laughter obviously caught some attention.

By the time Conrad had dumped Sonny off his float, the rest of the men were cheering, jumping with cannonball explosions into the water.

As they played and splashed like children, Conrad was glad for this break from reality. No. This wasn't reality. Not even close. It was surreal.

The adrenalin was gone and Conrad felt exhausted. A few of the guys lingered in the kitchen or the lounge, but Conrad needed sleep. He climbed the stairs gazing at the pool as he did with its hypnotic hazy lights.

Closing the door to his room, seeing no lock on it, Conrad knew he didn't mind a sneak visit from any of those guys, so he wouldn't have used a lock anyway. He needed a shower to wash off the chlorine from the pool. Before he stripped and braved the feeling of being naked and watched, Conrad picked up the diary camera and turned it on.

Pointing it at his face he whispered, “Day one. Had fun. I already know who’s going to end up a good friend and who I wish would be evicted.” He smiled. “Goodnight, Will and Charlotte.” He clicked it off and set it down on the dresser again.

Inside the bathroom, Conrad had a look at the camera. It was over the door pointing directly at the shower. “Perverts.” He dropped his damp shorts and stood over the sink in his briefs, brushing his teeth.

After finishing, he leaned into the tub and turned on the water. His attention kept being drawn to the camera lens behind him. Cursing under his breath, Conrad peeled down his briefs and climbed into the bathtub, closing the frosty curtain, knowing it provided limited coverage. Jacking off would be obvious, even if he faced his back to the camera.

He used the plastic wall dispensers which provided soap, shampoo and conditioner. Pumping shampoo into his palm and scrubbing up, he closed his eyes as he went through the men like a menu. Kelvin was an appetizer, his youth and blond ponytail, his innocence and charm, a nice start to a meal. Then Conrad imagined Alfonso. Using his tongue, Conrad would tease that belly-button ring and find the end of that heart tattoo. Lord knew how low the ink was drawn down Alfonso’s crotch.

Or maybe Dean…sampling the tattoo artist from Phoenix, staring into his deep brown eyes.

Sonny.

What could he say about Sonny? The man was perfection.

Tony? Tony would be the last bite of the meal. They’d arm wrestle to see who topped.

Conrad glanced down. His cock was sticking out from his body like a steel rod.

Using the soap dispenser, Conrad faced the tile wall and tried to conceal his movements. As slowly as he could, he whacked off, hoping the camera view through the steamy, frosted curtain was too blurry to see what he was doing. Luckily it didn't take long. He immediately rinsed and reached out for a towel before pushing back the curtain. Not making eye contact with the camera, Conrad dried off, nearly pressing his front against the door, trying to avoid the nosy lens.

Once he was through, he kept the towel around his hips until he was in bed under the blanket, falling fast asleep.

Chapter Three

Opening his eyes, it took a minute before Conrad realized where he was. He lay still, trying to focus before he moved. If he was at home he'd hop out of bed without a care. Here? He'd be showing off his morning erection to the universe.

Conrad checked the time on a digital clock on his nightstand. It was nearing eight. He reached to the floor for the towel he had used last night and sat up, wrapping it around his waist. Getting his clean clothing from the drawer, he closed himself into the bathroom and eyed the camera in frustration. Staring at the lens, Conrad took off the towel and raised it up to drape over the top of the camera.

"Uh uh…" came a chiding voice out of nowhere.

Conrad jumped in shock and wrapped the towel around his hips. He sat down on the toilet and caught his breath, the towel spread over his lap. A cold chill washed against his skin at the invasion of privacy. He didn't look up at the camera again, trying to use the towel to cover everything he did that he considered very private.

As Conrad headed down the stairs he could hear Alfonso's voice in the kitchen and smelled coffee.

"We should make a schedule," Alfonso said.

"I think it's a great idea."

Conrad stood at the threshold of the kitchen. Alfonso was speaking to Dean. Neither man was wearing a shirt.

"Mornin', Conrad." Dean smiled at him. "Did you sleep well?"

"Yes. Fine." Conrad approached Dean. "Holy shit. Look at you. You're a canvas." He wandered behind Dean's back to interpret the swirling colors and designs.

"I'm good for my business. Where's yours?"

"I don't have one. I think I'm the only housemate who doesn't."

"I'll change that." Dean grinned.

"There's coffee." Alfonso tilted his head towards the pot as he whipped a whisk in a bowl.

"Anyone need a topper?"

Dean held up his cup. "Thanks."

"Are we the only ones up?" Conrad tipped more coffee into Alfonso's mug too and sat next to Dean at the island counter after replacing the coffee pot.

"So far."

"Pancakes?" Conrad asked as he poured milk into his cup.

"Yes. Whole grain blueberry pancakes and low fat turkey sausages. They did do well making sure we're eating right. I don't know how Tony is going to react when he sees it's all health food."

"He doesn't look like he binges," Conrad said. "The guy's completely cut." After he sipped his coffee he noticed Alfonso and Dean staring at him.

"What?" Conrad felt that confusing cold pit in his stomach again and kept wondering why the fact that he could recognize a man who was fit was suspect.

"We were discussing the idea of a plan in the gym. I think the six of us in there at the same time is too much."

"We could split mornings and evenings." Conrad glanced

up. Sonny was standing there. Shirtless.

Conrad looked down at his t-shirt wondering if he missed that rule in the contract.

"Split it for what?" Sonny headed directly for the coffee and poured himself a cup. "Who needs a topper?"

"We're good." Dean raised his cup.

"Split for working out in the gym." Alfonso brought the bowl of pancake batter over to the electric griddle.

Sonny occupied the open stool next to Conrad. Conrad tried to be inconspicuous as he leaned in for a sniff of his aftershave or cologne.

"Yes, please. Six in that room is definitely a crowd." Sonny stared at Dean's arms. "I thought of doing that." He flexed his biceps, showing Dean his shoulder tattoo. "But just the thought of being eighty with that blue-smeared skin sagging down my arms turned me off."

"Augh!" Conrad recoiled in disgust. "What a thought!"

"Med school terror tactic?" Alfonso replied, using a ladle to drop blobs of batter on the griddle.

"Yeah. Maybe." Sonny chuckled.

"I'm not worried," Dean boasted, "I'll never sag."

Kelvin arrived next, his long, blond hair loose from the rubber band, as he yawned and scratched his smooth chest. The ultimate twink.

Conrad grew nervous. "Did the rules say you can't wear a shirt?"

"No." Sonny gave him a smirk. "Why?"

"Just that…" Conrad touched his t-shirt.

"You don't have to wear one, but there are no rules about it. Didn't you read the contract?" Kelvin poured the last of the coffee into a mug. "I better make more. Anyone know where the coffee grounds are?"

"Fridge. On the door." Alfonso flipped the pancakes.

"God knows what Tony is like without his caffeine in the morning." Kelvin rinsed the coffee pot.

Everyone laughed.

"I think I'm the only one who didn't dissect the fine print." Conrad finished his coffee.

"Never sign a contract without reading it." Dean stood and leaned near Alfonso, watching him cook. "I can tend the sausages."

"Thanks." Alfonso handed him a fork.

"Coffee…" someone moaned.

Conrad spun back to the door. Tony was there looking like a bear who'd been awaken early from his hibernation den.

"Making some. Chill." Kelvin flipped the switch on the automated machine.

"Bunch of hogs." He slumped over the counter on the stool Dean had been sitting on.

"Yeah, that's us. Oink." Conrad rolled his eyes at Sonny.

"Don't start with me, Con-man." Tony pointed his finger at him.

"Guys." Sonny threw up his hands. "It's not even nine."

"Pancakes are done."

"Sausages too." Dean shut off the stove.

Kelvin hustled over with a plate. "Any maple syrup?"

"There's low-fat butter and sugar-free syrup on the table." Alfonso pointed with his spatula.

"Did we luck out with a cook here or what?" Conrad held two plates up. "Here. Make a plate for yourself."

"Thanks, man." Alfonso piled pancakes on each dish.

"They plan that shit." Tony stuffed a wedge of pancake into his mouth as he sat at the dining room table.

"Oh?" Conrad asked, "What's your contribution?" Conrad used the maple syrup, passing it to Kelvin.

"My biting wit." Tony smiled, his mouth full.

Sonny choked and shook his head.

Will Markham's voice sounded over an invisible speaker. "Good morning, gentlemen."

He got a less than enthusiastic response. Conrad didn't stop eating, waving half-heartedly over his shoulder.

"Tony's contribution will be washing the dishes."

"Aw, come on!" Tony yelled at the ubiquitous voice.

Conrad enjoyed the chuckling at the table at the meted out punishment.

"What's the plan, Will?" Alfonso asked, looking directly at one camera.

"You shall see, gentlemen."

"Yeah, yeah." Dean muttered something under his breath.

"Don't like Will?" Conrad whispered.

"I like him as the producer of *Forever Young*. I don't know anything else about him. I'm hoping he's not a sadist."

They heard Will's laughter surround them.

Conrad shut up, as did everyone else. They caught eyes but didn't add to the conversation.

To Conrad's surprise, Tony didn't begrudge the task of loading the dishwasher. He did it tacitly as everyone handed him their plate and cleared up the rest of the items on the table.

The minute the kitchen was back in order, the front door opened.

Conrad stopped in his tracks as did the other five.

"Hello men!" Charlotte entered, appearing pert as usual. Behind her was a mob of people.

"What the fuck?" Conrad said before he realized it. He assumed they had a time delay and he would get a nice 'bleep' over his exclamation.

"May I introduce to you all Madison Henning." She made her now trademark, grand sweeping gesture with her arm. The cameras behind her were live with their red lights indicating recording like a lighthouse beacon.

A handsome man in his forties with dark hair, white at the temples, entered the foyer. He was dressed in LA chic, thong sandals, tanned to perfection, dark sunglasses, and off-white drawstring, linen pants with a matching traveler shirt, sleeves rolled up to the elbows.

Wow. Conrad knew Henning's work. Male nudes exclusively. The man reeked of wealth and power.

"Hello, boys."

Behind him a train of pretty studs entered the house, like silent calendar models.

Conrad's crotch went damp and hard. *Okay, this is a test, right? Weed out the gay guy? Is this the show's contest?*

"I'll show you to the pool, Madison." Charlotte led the entourage through the house as Conrad gaped at the assembly.

"Are they doing a photo shoot?" Sonny leaned against Conrad as he asked.

That woke Conrad up. "Looks like it."

Even though they weren't invited, the group of six housemates trailed behind the camera crew to the pool.

When Conrad made it outside, three of the models stripped down to g-string thongs.

Conrad had to stop drooling. He knew everything was being recorded and analyzed.

Madison was handed a camera by an assistant who was just as pretty as the boys, who were, 'wetting down' for their shot as Conrad ogled. *Oh, my, GOD! I can't watch this. I'm going to fricken come.*

Conrad gave his housemates a quick look. Though they all had poker faces on at the moment, they were riveted to the action.

"Okay!" Madison raised his camera to his eye level. "Show me some sex."

Conrad heard Sonny gulp in shock. Both Dean and Kelvin looked as if they were afraid to blink. No one made a comment about the fact that the shoot was of nearly naked men. Not even Tony uttered a sarcastic snipe.

Conrad expected someone to say aside, 'Geez, what's with the dudes? Can't we see naked women?'

Nope. Nothing. Are we all gay? Is that the joke?

Rubbing his forehead in agony, Conrad imagined having the balls to actually not watch. To enter the house, sit in the lounge, go lay in bed, have a nap, lift weights. But with the show going on in front of him of nearly nude, gorgeous young men, all with large semi-erections exposed from saturated triangles of fabric, Conrad wasn't going anywhere.

Instead, he plopped down on a chaise lounge and tried to catch his breath. Sonny shoved Conrad's legs over and landed heavily at the foot, his eyes never leaving the action.

One by one the housemates seemed to drop like a lead sack onto a chair and gape silently as full packages were nearly exposed, massaged and thrust out for Madison's hungry camera lens.

Conrad forced himself to stop panting and noticed Charlotte's wry smirk. *Some game, Ms. Deavers. A very wicked game. Come out on a reality show. That's the purpose. Take six guys who are gay, not out, and torment them sexually until they either admit it, or seduce another housemate. That has to be it. Son of a bitch!*

"Nice, Hans!" Madison sank to one knee, aiming his camera at the young man's groin. "Stick your hand into your suit."

Conrad closed his eyes and didn't watch. It didn't matter. His imagination gave him a vivid picture. *I can't sit here.* He was about to get up and leave, get a bottle of water, anything to stop this tease when Sonny leaned on his leg. Holding his breath, Conrad blinked as he judged the contact. It was so subtle it could have been accidental. But Sonny must feel the heat and sweat coming from his leg. *I'm not moving*. But he was glad for the distraction. Sonny may not be a Swedish model, but he was exactly the kind of man Conrad wanted in his life.

"That's it, Georg! Rub yourself. Nice." Madison obviously was enjoying his work. "Embrace Nils. Good. Push your hips together."

Kelvin was the first to surrender. He seemed to climb off the lounge chair as if he were eighty, not twenty-one. He vanished into the house. To Conrad's astonishment, Tony was next.

Alfonso and Dean watched the men's exit. Conrad witnessed the two men exchange glances, then they too entered the house.

"I need water," Conrad said to Sonny.

"Me too." Sonny rose up, and for a second he appeared to want to extend his hand to help Conrad stand, reconsidering and entering the house. Conrad was the last to avoid the erotic show outside, walking to the kitchen where the group had gathered. Sonny opened the fridge, and when he handed Conrad a bottle of water, everyone asked for one.

After he drank, Tony said, "What the hell was that about? Do we need to see stupid trophy-airheads pose like that?"

"No." Kelvin didn't meet anyone's eye.

Though Conrad suspected the ruse, he wasn't about to verbalize it.

Dean rubbed his own arms as if he were chilly. "That actually sucked."

"Yeah, it did." Alfonso curled his lip as he spoke. Everyone appeared upset.

Since no one was left to play the voyeur, the photo shoot

ended. Charlotte escorted the models out of the house and kissed Madison on the cheek. "Thank you, sweetie. Always a pleasure."

Madison handed his camera off to his assistant. "Too bad you boys left. I wanted to include you in my new book."

"That's just what I need," Conrad replied under his breath.

"Me too," Tony said. "I teach, remember?"

Madison held up his hands in defense and waved. "Good luck with the rest of the stay."

Once he was gone, Charlotte whispered into the cameraman's ear. He nodded and left as well. She approached the group with an exaggerated pout. "I'm disappointed. I thought I was giving you guys some entertainment to ease your boredom."

"How about a Wii instead?" Kelvin did not smile.

"I'll take an iPod." Sonny crushed the empty water bottle in his fist.

"Now, now." She wagged her finger.

The front door opened and two men entered carrying large, cardboard boxes. They propped them up on the counter and left without a word.

"See you boys tomorrow!" Charlotte waved and left with the rest of her crew.

Alfonso was the first to cross the room and open the flap of a box. "Booze."

"Yes." Dean pumped his fist.

Conrad watched as Alfonso removed an enormous quantity of premium micro-brews and hard liquor. "Uh oh. We're so fucked."

"No kidding." Sonny shook his head. "Uh, guys, they want us to get wasted and act like morons."

"They got their wish." Tony cracked open the tequila and drank it from the bottle.

"Food too." Alfonso began stacking things on the counter.

"What's on the menu, chef?" Dean walked closer to look over Alfonso's shoulder.

Conrad noticed Dean place his hand on Alfonso's arm as he did. Now *that* turned Conrad on.

"Let's see…shrimp…scallops…nice!" Alfonso held up a plastic bag. "Leeks, fresh garlic, romaine, red onions, grape tomatoes… Delish!"

"Any potato chips?" Kelvin pushed through the bags of food and alcohol.

"Sorry." Dean petted Kelvin's long blond hair affectionately.

"Darn."

Conrad lit up like a sparkler stick. *Are we getting that cozy we can touch each other? Is that okay?*

"We need to eat lunch." Sonny began loading the perishable food into the refrigerator. "Tony. Stop drinking that."

"Yeah." He gulped a last mouthful and capped it. "Later."

"Anything edible for lunch?" Kelvin rubbed his stomach.

Alfonso gave him a sweet smile. "Is this weaning you off junk food?"

"Shit yeah. I'm craving sugar and salt so badly I'm in withdrawal." Kelvin laughed but it wasn't jubilant.

"Here." Alfonso handed him a yoghurt cup. "Fruit on the bottom."

"Are you serious?" Kelvin held it up. "Yech. It says 'fat free'."

"It'll help kill your sugar craving."

"Fucking girl-food. I don't eat yoghurt."

"Eat it." Dean handed Kelvin a spoon. "Try it, you'll like it."

"This is how desperate I am." He waved his spoon in

defiance and flopped down on a stool, peeling the lid back.

"He's really charming," Sonny whispered to Conrad.

Overriding his jealous impulse, Conrad replied, "Yeah, he is. Like a kid brother."

"Exactly." Sonny winked.

Conrad stretched in front of the mirrors in their house-bound gym with Sonny and Kelvin accompanying him. Outdoors he could see the other three lying in the sunshine on lounge chairs or floating in the pool.

Though Conrad wouldn't have complained about who was chosen to workout with him, he was very happy with the choice. Alfonso appeared to take the lead in most decisions, and since Conrad agreed with him, he didn't mind. The fitness trainer from Orange County never made him feel as if he was being bossy or competitive. Alfonso was just a natural at guiding them, which made sense since he helped people change their lifestyles for the better.

Sonny, in his sexy football pants, loaded up a bar for squats while Kelvin sprinted away, running on the treadmill.

For no rational reason, Conrad thought about the man he had left behind in California. John. It was painful. Nothing was worse than being dumped. *Open relationship? I'm supposed to agree to being in an open relationship? No. I'm not that kind of man. I need a one-man man.*

Conrad wondered if that incident was the main reason he'd opted for this reality gig. Was it a way to show himself he was worth keeping and not letting go? He was a man in his prime, loyal, trustworthy. So he was between jobs. That didn't mean he was unemployable. The construction industry was suffering in every state.

"Conrad?"

"Huh?" He woke up.

"Could you just spot me for one? There's no squat rack."

"Oh. Yes. Sorry." Conrad walked behind Sonny, facing the mirrors.

Sonny crouched in front of a loaded bar of weights and rubbed his gloves over the textured metal to get a sure hold. He nodded he was ready.

Conrad stood by as Sonny hefted the load to his shoulders, stood under the burden, and widened his stance.

"How many?"

"One. Two if I can."

Conrad nodded, reaching out to the bar without touching it. Sonny squatted down and roared to get back to upright. Though Conrad had the urge to grab the bar, he waited. Sonny stood vertically, gasping for breath and shifting the enormous load which pressed behind his neck.

"I'll need your help but I'm doing another."

"Okay."

Sonny nodded he was going for it.

Conrad placed both hands on the bar but did nothing to help yet. Sonny slowly lowered down and Conrad could feel him strain right through the metal. He felt Sonny struggling to stand and gave the weights the small hoist Sonny needed to get back upright. "Get it off me."

Conrad strained to lift the bar from Sonny's shoulders and set it down on the floor. As he eyed it, he counted up the weight. "I'm impressed."

"Don't be. My brother can do that weight to warm up." Sonny stretched his back and neck, shaking off the pain.

"Is he a med student too?"

"No. Linebacker with the Eagles."

"Really?" Kelvin gripped the side rails of the treadmill as he ran, gaping at Sonny.

"Really." Sonny crouched down, looking dizzy or lightheaded.

Conrad knelt next to him, rubbing his sweaty back. “Put your head between your knees.”

“I’m all right. Give me a minute.”

“We need more carbs.” Conrad looked up at the camera and yelled, “We need carbs, Will!”

He waited for a reply but none came. That didn’t mean he wasn’t heard. “They got us on protein, fruit and veggies.”

“We had carbs for breakfast.”

Conrad remembered the pancakes. “Right.” He kept massaging Sonny’s upper back. “You need help sitting on the bench? I can get you to the bench.”

“I’ll be okay. That feels nice.”

Blinking in surprise, Conrad looked into the reflection and spotted Kelvin watching curiously. Of course the cameras didn’t miss a thing either. That made Conrad self-conscious. “Come on.” He held Sonny’s arm and stood him up, walking him to the bench. When he had Sonny sitting, Conrad spun around. Three men were standing at the back window, hands shading the glare, staring in.

“Jesus!” Conrad laughed. He approached the glass and mouthed, “He’s okay.”

Alfonso gave Conrad a thumbs up, like he’d understood. Dean nodded, and Tony grinned wickedly and grabbed his crotch in a provocative gesture.

Conrad flipped him off, but smiled as he did.

Tony laughed and walked back to the lounge chairs.

Kelvin shut down the treadmill. “Well, it ain’t Big Brother, but I feel like we each have five of them.”

“Yeah,” Sonny said, still catching his breath. “It’s nice. I like it.”

Conrad sat next to Sonny and leaned their sweaty shoulders together. “Me too.”

Sonny met his eyes and smiled.

The one thing no one complained about was the evening meal. Alfonso's creations and the fresh ingredients were satisfying.

After the voice of Will Markham commanded Kelvin to do kitchen clean-up, everyone pitched in and helped anyway.

Six men, with either a beer or a shot of tequila, or both in their hands, slouched in the lounge at the front of the house and relaxed.

Conrad sat next to Sonny, one leg tucked under him, a frosty micro-brew to sip. He was thinking this living arrangement was too good to be true and three weeks wasn't enough.

"I used to teach tennis at a club in Sacramento." Alfonso drank his beer from the bottle. He wiped his mouth with the back of his hand before he continued. "I was involved with a scandal involving a senator and his wife."

Tony snickered, downing an unknown number of tequila shooters. Conrad had lost count.

Kelvin asked, "You cheated with her on the senator?"

"Yeah." Alfonso laughed softly. "It was stupid. She turned out to be pretty horrible."

The thought of them all being gay just went out of the window. Conrad shifted slightly away from Sonny.

Sonny noticed it. "You need more room?"

"I'm okay." Conrad didn't want any attention drawn to him and Sonny at the moment. "Which senator?"

Alfonso drank his beer, making a loud banging noise with the bottle on the table as if finishing it was triumphant. "Kipp Kensington."

"No!" Dean gasped. "The staunch Republican who ended up with that biker?"

"What? What biker?" Kelvin sat up. "Who? What

happened?"

"Don't you watch the news?" Sonny asked, putting his arm on the back of the sofa behind Conrad.

Instantly Conrad began to sweat as if the act would label him gay.

"I sort of do." Kelvin shrugged, twirling his ponytail in one finger.

Dean said, "Kipp Kensington came out. He was marching in a gay pride event and announced he was gay and involved with this biker guy."

"The biker's name was Robin Grant." Sonny smiled. "The senator was like ten years older than Robin too."

"It was a huge upset to the Republican party at the time." Alfonso stood, stretching, his shirt parted revealing his tattoo and navel jewelry.

Conrad tried not to stare.

"More booze?" he asked as he collected bottles.

"Yes please!" Everyone answered.

Tony laughed. "You had to ask?"

"No more for you." Dean pointed to Tony. "You're drunk."

"Fuck you. I know my limit, and I ain't driving, am I?"

"You get sick, you clean it up." Sonny climbed off the couch. "I'll help you, Alfonso."

"Thanks, man."

Conrad admired Sonny's ass as he left the room. Since it was a constant seventy-five degrees in the house, everyone was either shirtless, or in tiny tank tops and shorts.

As Sonny vanished across the hall, Conrad connected to Tony's gaze. His stomach pinched at the look he was receiving.

"You checking out Sonny's butt?"

"No." Conrad tried to make light of it. "Are you?"

"That's an infantile evasion."

"Shut up." Conrad tried to control his temper. "Please tell me you don't really teach children."

"Yup. I do." Tony stretched his arms over his head, showing off large rolling biceps.

"What grade?" Kelvin asked.

Since Tony was seated next to Kelvin on a couch, Tony leaned his elbow on the back of it and rested his chin on his palm. "Your age, baby-boy."

"I'm twenty-one!" Kelvin appeared indignant.

"No, really, Tony," Dean asked, "What grade?"

"Third."

"Turd?" Conrad mocked Tony's thick accent.

"Okay, hot shot, what the hell do you do, other than, *used to* work in construction?" Tony shifted his position and propped his bare feet on the coffee table. "You even got a job?"

"Not at the moment. Christ, I can't believe you remember that." Conrad sat up as Alfonso and Sonny returned with more alcohol.

"Need potato chips. I'm dyin'." Kelvin reached out for a bottle of beer.

"Go look. I haven't checked every cabinet." Alfonso sat in his spot on a chair with an ottoman.

Kelvin leapt up and Conrad could hear doors opening and closing in the kitchen.

"So, the unemployed tool man is talking shit to a teacher." Tony drank his beer. "Sad, baby, very sad."

"What did we miss?" Sonny returned to his place on the sofa.

Tony said, "Conny is unemployed but still thinks it's nice to taunt me. Right, Conny?"

"Screw you." Conrad didn't need this shit.

Kelvin stood at the threshold of the room, holding out a plastic bag. "I got nuts."

Dean immediately choked on his beer. Sonny exchanged glances with Conrad, and Alfonso rolled in his chair he was laughing so hard.

"Let's see em', baby." Tony grinned devilishly.

The expression of bewilderment on Kelvin's face was priceless to Conrad. "Oh, Kelvin, you are the best of the bunch."

Kelvin sat where he had been. "No seriously, guys, what did I say?" He tried to hand Tony the bag of peanuts. "Here."

"Never mind." Tony ran his hand over the top of his head, indicating the joke went over Kelvin's.

"Anyway…" Dean coughed and sat up in his chair.

"Hey, Deano, I was thinking of getting a Harley tat."

"Wings?"

"Yeah."

"Where?"

"I don't know. Maybe my low back."

"Cool."

Conrad asked Sonny, "How many tattoos do you have?"

"Why?" Sonny's smile was full of invitation.

"Just curious." Conrad drank his beer and noticed all the other men were staring at him. "What?"

"You got tat-envy, Conny?"

"I got one." Kelvin dropped the bag of peanuts on the coffee table, hopped to his feet and pulled his gym shorts down in front.

Conrad thought for a minute they were in for a free peek of full frontal.

"Here." Kelvin kept his cock covered, revealing shaved pubic hair and a tattoo that read 'carpe diem' near the base of his cock. He pivoted around to make sure everyone could see it.

"Nice, baby. Very nice." Tony's smiled, showing his perfect white teeth. "That makes Conny the only tattoo virgin."

"I can change that." Dean gave Conrad the same wicked smile Tony had given Kelvin. "A day with me, Conrad, and you'll no longer be a virgin."

What the fuck? Conrad knew he was getting drunk and assumed the other men were slowly degenerating into a state of inebriation as well.

"I doubt very much Conrad is a virgin."

Conrad whipped his head around to Sonny at the comment. "Are we still talking about tattoos?"

"Anyone want my nuts?" Kelvin offered the bag.

Alfonso physically fell out of the chair and sat on the floor choking with laughter.

"Is that funny too?" Kelvin blinked.

Conrad asked Sonny in a whisper, "Am I hearing this shit for real?"

Sonny shrugged but the look in his eyes was pure sexual.

"Fine." Kelvin curled up on the couch with his snack. "I'll keep my nuts to myself."

That line made Alfonso roar with hilarity and pound the floor. "Oh, God! Help. I'm in pain!"

Dean kept coughing from inhaling his beer down the wrong pipe as he cracked up and Tony was wiping his eyes as they ran with tears.

Seeing poor Kelvin bewildered, Conrad said, "Nuts? As is ball sack?"

The light turned on in Kelvin's eyes. "Oh!"

"He's precious." Sonny dabbed at the corner of his eye as he laughed.

"As a little brother." Conrad stopped smiling.

Sonny reached out and squeezed Conrad's leg. "As a kid brother."

Alfonso crawled back onto his chair like a cat on catnip.

"I want your nuts," Tony said to Kelvin.

Kelvin reached out with the bag.

"No. Not those, baby."

"Ha. Ha." Kelvin retracted his arm.

"Oh, man." Alfonso composed himself. "This is why I never drink. I'm a cheap drunk."

"Are you drunk?" Dean asked with a gleam to his eye.

"Yeah, why? You intending on taking advantage of me?"

Conrad looked up at the camera. Did they forget about it? He didn't.

"Why?" Dean played the game. "Are you easy when you're drunk?"

"Louise Kensington thought so." Alfonso propped his feet back on the ottoman. "Fucker was an alcoholic and tried to get me to be one." He finished his beer and slammed it on the table like he had with the first one. "Done. Before I get stupid."

"Or horny?" Dean grinned.

Conrad could see Dean was attracted to Alfonso. Who wouldn't be? The guy was gorgeous. Was Dean gay? Was it a fifty-fifty ratio of gay men to straight men? Was that the contest here?

"I'm always horny."

"Uh, guys." Conrad pointed to the camera.

"What's wrong, Conny? Men aren't supposed to get horny?"

"Whatever, man." Conrad shut up. He wasn't about to go head to head with the man from the Bronx on international television and the web.

Kelvin tossed the bag of peanuts on the coffee table and

hugged his beer. "Ya can't even do yourself in this place without a camera watching."

"I have." Sonny grinned wickedly.

Conrad felt his cock throb at the thought of Sonny playing with his dick. He rubbed his face as he began to feel self-consciously about his erection.

"Yeah?" Dean appeared as interested in Sonny as Conrad was. But at the moment, they were all drunk. "Where?"

"Under cover." Sonny stuck his tongue out at the camera.

Alfonso said, "Ditto," as he stuffed both his hands into the front of his shorts.

"In the shower," Tony boasted. "They want to watch me spank my monkey? Go ahead."

Dean grinned. "In the closet."

"Facing the camera?" Alfonso asked.

"Nope. Back to it. I'm not as bold as our Italian stallion."

"He isn't the only Italian stallion in the room, *bello*." Alfonso gave Dean a wicked smirk.

"Do you speak Italian?" Tony looked impressed.

"I do. Both my parents are from Florence. I grew up speaking it. I had to work like hell to get rid of the accent."

"What did ya do that for, ya dick?" Tony finished his beer.

Alfonso shrugged. "Living in the O.C. It rubbed off."

"Looks like you're about to 'rub off'." Sonny tilted his head to where Alfonso's hands were.

"So?" Kelvin asked, "I'm the only schmuck who didn't jack off last night?"

All eyes came to rest of Conrad.

He cleared his throat and glanced at the camera. "Will? Shut the thing off for one minute, okay?"

"Not on your life," the booming voice reminded them they were not alone.

Alfonso flipped his hands quickly out of his pants.

"Conrad pleasured himself in the shower, boys," Will announced.

Scrubbing his face in embarrassment, Conrad replied, "Thanks, Will."

"Anytime, Conrad."

Sonny chuckled. "Yes. Just you, Kelvin."

"Shit." Kelvin shifted in his seat. "I'm doing it tonight."

"What the hell are you embarrassed about, Conny?" Tony grabbed his own crotch. "Men. We're fucking men. Are you a man, Conny?"

"Come on, Tony." Sonny shifted his position on the couch. "Don't pick on him."

"Can't he defend himself?" Tony asked, blinking his eyes as if he were innocent. "You need the med student to fight your battles, Conny?"

Conrad stared at Tony. It was silent around him, but he knew everyone was watching, including the world. "Why is it there is always one?"

"One what?" Tony stuck out his chest.

"One ass."

Flying to his feet, Tony got into a fighting stance. "Come on." He waved his hand.

Sonny held Conrad's arm, as if holding him back.

"Come on!" Tony gestured, opening himself up.

Conrad wanted to. He wanted to beat the crap out of Tony, but not for the reasons the others assumed. Conrad had pent up hostility from his break up in Elk Grove. He didn't give a crap about some bully from the Bronx.

"Fucking figured," Tony mocked him, crossing his arms. "Sissy-shit."

Before Conrad could think, he flew off the couch and slammed Tony into the wall. The look on Tony's face was pure shock. But it only took a second for Tony to recover. He grappled with Conrad, trying to push him off.

"Tough now, Tony? Tough now?" Conrad was seething, nearly blind with rage as he envisioned the man he really wanted to pummel.

Just before Tony swung back for a punch, Dean was there, holding Tony's wrist. Conrad felt arms around his waist, pulling him backwards.

Calming down, Conrad was about to release his hold on Tony when he felt Tony grind a thick cock into his. Conrad nearly fell over from the surprise. He instantly let go and backed up. Tony appeared sheepish for a moment, as if he had revealed his fatal flaw.

"Get this piece of shit away from me," Tony said, shaking off Dean's hold.

Everyone was on their feet but Alfonso. He was smirking as he relaxed in his chair. "Ah, gentlemen. You fell right into their trap. Booze and bravado make excellent bed-fellows. And on that note, goodnight." He got up and walked out of the room, not looking back.

Kelvin backed out of the room, as if it would ignite from the bad vibes.

Will's voice commanded, "Conrad, clean up the empty bottles and get the house back to perfection."

Tony sneered in pleasure and left.

"I'll help you," Sonny picked up an empty beer bottle.

"Go to bed, Sonny," Will ordered.

As if Sonny were about to protest, he opened his mouth and faced the camera. Conrad touched his arm. "Go."

"Sorry, babe." Sonny put the bottle down.

Hearing the other housemates climb the stairs, Conrad took a moment to control himself. Inhaling deeply, he thought about his own lingering anger over his break up, Sonny's affection, and of course, Tony's excitement over being physical with him. Three gay? *Me, Tony, and...who?*

Chapter Four

Brushing his teeth, staring at his reflection, Conrad gazed at his blue eyes and naturally-highlighted, dishwater-blond hair. He spat out the toothpaste and rinsed his mouth. His gaze was drawn to the camera that was mounted above the door between the ceiling and the trim. “Morning, Will.”

He waited. No reply.

Once he had finished his morning routine, including shaving, and moisturizing his face, Conrad opened his bedroom door. Noise from the floor below reached his ears, but it wasn’t just the sound of his five housemates. It was again loud enough to indicate they were in for something unusual.

Making his way down the slatted stairs, Conrad paused halfway and watched large television camera being wheeled onto the back patio. “Oh no. Now what? Aren’t we already on TV?”

Straightening his posture and continuing down the stairs, Conrad ignored the commotion and located Alfonso and Dean in the kitchen drinking coffee. “Morning.”

“Hi, Conrad.” Dean smiled.

As he poured himself a cup, Conrad asked, “Anyone have any idea?” and tilted his head in the direction of the chaos.

“All we can garner is that there’s going to be some kind of shoot. We have no clue what it’s about.” Alfonso sipped his coffee.

"Has Charlotte shown yet?" Conrad tipped milk into his mug.

"Speak of the devil." Dean's eyes darted behind Conrad's back.

"I resent that!" Charlotte laughed. "I'm not the devil, I only do his bidding." She glanced around the kitchen. "Where's the rest of the boys?"

"Sleeping?" Alfonso replied.

"You." She pointed to Dean, "Wake up Tony the Tiger…You." She aimed her loaded finger at Alfonso. "Wake up babycakes-Kelvin…and you…" She smiled so wickedly Conrad felt a chill up his spine. "Wake sexy Sonny."

Cold sweat coated Conrad. Somehow he must have exposed how much he liked Sonny. Either that or Charlotte was a very good guesser.

"Now! Chop, chop!" She clapped.

Conrad placed his mug on the counter and hustled out, jogging down the hall, up the stairs.

"Why do I get stuck with Tony?" Dean grumbled.

"She'd be nuts to ask me." Conrad stopped short at the top landing and Alfonso slammed into him.

"What?" Alfonso asked.

Conrad touched his lip as he thought about it. *Where was Sonny's bedroom?*

As if reading his mind, Alfonso pushed him in the direction. "Last door on the left."

"I should know that." Conrad laughed at himself and heard the other two chuckle. "No. Maybe I shouldn't." He walked down the hall without looking back.

Pressing his ear to the door, he knocked. "Sonny?" Behind him he heard Dean and Alfonso doing the same with their tasks. He called Sonny's name once more and then opened the door.

As he entered the bedroom, which was exactly like his own, Conrad spotted Sonny asleep on the bed. His body was exposed enough so that Conrad was able to see one of the tattoos Sonny didn't admit he had. Over the top of Sonny's butt was a scrolling thin line, like barbed wire. And the sheet was low enough to see the origin of Sonny's perfect ass crack and cheeks.

"Holy shit." Conrad's cock thickened in his shorts. Cameras. Cameras. Everywhere.

"Sonny?" he whispered, stepping closer. "Sonny?"

As if he just heard him, Sonny jerked his head up and spun around, startled.

The glimpse of Sonny's semi-hard cock had Conrad about to spurt. "Sorry, man. Charlotte sent me up here to wake you." Conrad could not keep eye contact if his life depended on it. Another tattoo became visible. One on the side of Sonny's cock. It was tiny and Conrad could not discern it from where he stood, though he tried.

Sonny yanked up the sheet and Conrad woke out of his daydream.

"Okay." Conrad held up both hands. "All I had to do was make sure you're awake. See ya down there." He left, closing the door behind him and jogged back to the kitchen, once again stopping on the stairs to see what could possibly be going on out by the pool this time. *We already had a model shoot. What now?*

Alfonso and Dean ended up behind him. Alfonso put his hand on Conrad's shoulder. "What the hell are they doing out there?"

"If I had to guess?" Dean leaned closer. "I'd say they're going to shoot a commercial or something. At least Charlotte's out of our hair for a moment."

"Oh, no." Alfonso moaned. "Not more Swedish models with monster marble bags."

Conrad cracked up with laughter and continued down the stairs. He picked up his coffee, hoping it was still warm.

"Food." Alfonso opened the refrigerator and removed a carton of eggs and a loaf of seeded bread.

"You don't have to be the one cooking all the time." Conrad refreshed all three of their cups.

"I love it." Alfonso placed a frying pan on the stove top. "How do you like your eggs?"

"Sunny side up." Conrad replaced the coffee carafe.

"How appropriate." Dean dropped four slices of toast in the toaster.

"Don't you start on me." Conrad sank in spirit.

Once Dean lowered the bread into the coils, he stood in front of Conrad and cupped his jaw. "I'm kidding, babe."

Conrad's breath caught in his throat and his body went into meltdown. He couldn't stop panting. "You're not going to kiss me, are you, Dean?"

"No. Why? Want me to?"

"Ah hum?" Alfonso glanced over his shoulder as he heated the frying pan.

"Jealous?"

"Hell yeah!" Alfonso laughed and cracked an egg into a bowl. "Let me guess, Dean, scrambled."

"That'll work." Dean picked up his coffee cup and sipped it.

Right before Conrad could whisper, Are you guys gay? Kelvin scuffed in. "Coffee…coffee…"

"Hung over, baby?" Dean tugged on Kelvin's ponytail.

"Uh. Yes?" Kelvin cringed. "Ow?" He massaged his temples and dragged his heels to the counter, pouring a cup of coffee.

"Eggs?" Alfonso asked Kelvin as the toast popped and Dean replaced the four slices with four more.

"Ew. No. What's going on outside?" Kelvin sipped his black coffee, made a face in disgust and stirred in milk and sugar. "Who made the gasoline?"

"I did." Dean laughed, sliding the lever on the next four slices of bread.

Conrad located a butter-like spread and began coating the toast.

"How are your nuts?" Alfonso asked.

"Better. Thanks." Kelvin sat down on a stool.

Conrad glanced at him from over his shoulder. "Under cover?"

"Yeah. Slept on the wet spot. Sucked."

"Use something!" Dean began laughing uncontrollably.

"Like what?"

"I don't know? A tissue?" Dean dabbed at his eyes and couldn't stop laughing.

"What now?" Sonny asked as he came in the room.

Dean said, "Kelvin worked his nuts under cover and made a mess."

"Dean!" Kelvin turned a lovely shade of red.

A voice over the speakers said, "Kelvin."

"Oh crap." Kelvin looked like the Cowardly Lion when the Wizard called his name. "Yes, Will?"

"Strip all the beds and do the laundry."

"Groan!" Kelvin yelled back.

Conrad winked at Sonny in reaction to the punishment.

Dean cuddled Kelvin from behind and pressed his cheek against Kelvin's. "Sorry, baby. I'll help."

"You'll iron," Will announced.

"Groan!" Dean stood straight and replied to the camera in annoyance.

"Ha. Ha." Kelvin stuck out his tongue at Dean.

Alfonso was hysterical with laughter again. “I love it here.” He used the spatula to divvy up the eggs. “Sunny-side up and scrambled.”

“Thanks.” Conrad took two slices of the buttered toast and sat at the table.

“Sonny? You want eggs?” Alfonso asked.

“Sure. Any style.” He poured coffee for himself and filled the carafe for a fresh pot.

“What the fuck’s going on outside?” Tony entered the room and took a mug from the cabinet.

“No one knows.” Dean sat next to Conrad to eat his breakfast.

“Always have to wait for a fresh pot to brew.” Tony grumbled. “You making eggs? I want mine poached.”

“Fried or scrambled,” Alfonso replied. “You want them poached, you make them.”

“Who got you up on the wrong side of the bed?”

“You.” Alfonso handed Sonny a plate of eggs. “Toast popped. Grab a slice.”

“Thanks, man.” Sonny took the plate and buttered two. “Kelvin? Toast?”

“Do we have jelly or peanut butter?”

“Again with the nuts?” Tony took the coffee pot before it finished dripping and filled a mug with the contents. “How many nuts do you need to make you happy?”

“Leave the kid alone.” Sonny sat across from Conrad and began eating.

“He should do the laundry.” Kelvin pointed to Tony. He used the imitation butter on the bread and made a sour face. “Bet this sucks.”

“It’s not too bad.” Alfonso shut off the burner and took a plate to the table for himself.

“Where’s mine?” Tony asked.

"Poach your own eggs." Alfonso didn't look at Tony.

Tony muttered under his breath and stuck more bread into the toaster.

"You clean the kitchen, Tony."

"Come on, Will!" Tony yelled at the camera. "I always get clean up."

"You want to iron the sheets?" Dean asked.

"Iron what?" Tony knotted the end of the plastic bag of bread and tossed it on the counter.

"I'm doing laundry and Dean's ironing the sheets. You want to swap?" Kelvin sat at the table with the others.

Tony ignored him.

"Didn't think so." Dean kept eating.

Conrad met Sonny's eye and caught his smile. "Hey, good boy. You haven't gotten a chore yet."

"Shh." Sonny put his finger to his lips.

By late afternoon, Conrad stood, arms crossed, at the back sliding door staring at the multitude of cameras, sound equipment, spotlights and men who were connecting wires to monitors and control panels. Warmth mingled over his back.

Sonny whispered, "They talking?"

"Not a word. My guess is Charlotte threatened them with castration if they spilled." Conrad felt Sonny's body press against his bottom. The urge to wriggle back was overwhelming. He resisted, trying to feel if Sonny was excited.

"What the hell can it be? It's got to be a commercial. You think they're going to pick one of us for it?"

"I have no idea. Would you do it?"

"Depends. If it's for a penile enhancement product? No."

When Sonny laughed, Conrad felt his breath move his hair. "Bet you don't need any of that."

"At twenty-five I better not."

Conrad closed his eyes and savored Sonny's contact.

"Going to sleep?" Alfonso leaned against Conrad's side, pressing his arms against the glass sliding door.

His eyes springing open, Conrad cleared his throat. "No. Uh, so, anyone know what's going on out there?" With two fabulous men making contact with him, Conrad was about to blow his cover, and/or spunk, over one of them.

Kelvin snuck under Sonny and in front of Conrad so he could see. Suddenly three men were sandwiching Conrad.

"What did they say? Did anyone ask the working men anything?" Kelvin said.

"They're not talking." Conrad inhaled. Men. Cologne. Pheromones…stimulating the hell out of him.

"No?" Kelvin looked up at Conrad's height. "You asked one of them?"

"Yes."

Sonny leaned his chin on Conrad's shoulder. Conrad nearly passed out. When Conrad's cock throbbed against Kelvin from Sonny's actions, Kelvin first looked down at Conrad's body, then up at his face.

Conrad felt his cheeks go hot.

Dean joined the group, pressed against Alfonso from behind, beside Conrad and Sonny. "Any idea yet?"

No matter what, Conrad could not stop his cock from pulsating, and the way Kelvin was standing, it was moving directly into Kelvin's hip. Conrad mustered up courage and looked into Kelvin's eyes. He was grinning like he knew Conrad's secret. And perhaps he now did.

"What the hell?" Tony asked. "Did you go out and ask those monkeys what's going on? Or are you all just standing here like hungry brats with your noses pressed to a candy store window?"

Conrad tried to open the door but there were too many bodies in his way. He was so humiliated Kelvin knew he was hard, he was beginning to sweat. "I can't get out."

"You sure you want to?" Kelvin smiled.

"What did he say?" Tony asked.

"Oh God help me." Conrad dragged the slider back with a powerful tug and the group toppled out onto the patio.

Tony swaggered over to one of the workmen. "Okay, fess up or I'll get violent."

The man laughed at him and continued to plug in cords.

Alfonso grabbed Tony from behind and pushed him away from the man. "Sit down. You teach children? That's got to be bullshit."

"Boys!" Charlotte made a grand entrance from the house. "Sit! Sit!"

Conrad relaxed on a lounge and Kelvin practically sat on his lap. Quickly Conrad backed up and straddled the chair so Kelvin's bottom was not on his groin. Kelvin gave Conrad a coy, bat of his eyelashes.

No, it was not you I was getting a hard-on for! Okay, who's gay? Me and Dean? And Kelvin? Tony? Sonny? Who's gay? Is that the catch? All of us? All but one?

Conrad caught Sonny's curious gaze and shrugged like he had no clue why Kelvin had decided to get cozy.

Kelvin leaned his back against Conrad's chest.

"What are you doing?" Conrad whispered.

"Nuthin'." Kelvin rested his arms on Conrad's thighs.

"What's the deal, Char?" Tony threw up his hands. "Cameras, lights? Who's the star? I'm hoping it's me."

"Oh, sweetie..." She squeezed Tony's face until she puckered his lips. "No. I have a bigger treat for my boys."

He backed out of her grip and glared at her.

"Augh!" Kelvin sat up and gasped.

It gave Conrad a heart attack because he didn't know why, and dreaded it being because Kelvin was sensing his cock moving again.

When two men stepped out of the house, Conrad felt goose bumps rise on his arms. Kelvin sprung out of the lounge chair and nearly swooned in a dramatic gesture, like Maureen O'Hara in *Gone With the Wind*. "Keith O'Leary and Carl Bronson! Oh, my God! Oh, my God! You're my favorite stars!"

"Could you act more gay, Kelvy?" Tony sneered. "Take a breath before you cream yourself."

"Shut up." Alfonso snarled at Tony.

Being polite, Conrad got to his feet and felt his throat go dry. He wasn't a big celebrity chaser. He didn't read the gossip rags or fawn over who did what in Hollywood, but…

These guys were different. It was as if when they entered the patio, the air rippled with a blast of a bomb. Their aura was very powerful.

As Charlotte introduced them, Conrad extended his hand and shook each one, saying something mundane, like 'Nice to meet you'. He didn't remember a minute later.

"Do you watch *Forever Young*?" Sonny asked, pressing his lips against Conrad's ear to make sure it was not overheard.

"Doesn't everyone?"

"What do you think of their sex scenes?"

Conrad turned to look Sonny in the eye. He had no idea how to answer him.

"We're going to film a scene for the television show," Charlotte said, rubbing her hands together. "Huh? How cool is that? Are we smart here at *Got Men?* or what?"

Kelvin was gaping at the stars as if he was in the presence of royalty. Conrad overheard him ask Charlotte, "Can we get our photos taken with them? Huh? Or an autograph?"

"Sure, sweetie-pie." She pinched Kelvin's cheek.

"How are you men surviving?" Carl asked.

"Good." Dean nodded.

"Except when Will Markham decides to punish us." Alfonso appeared so comfortable with the famous men, Conrad envied him.

"He is a martyr that way." Keith winked. "The first few sex scenes Carl and I did were murder." Keith grinned at Charlotte. "Right, Ms. Deavers?"

"Got you both Emmys so quit whining." She laughed.

Kelvin made a bold step closer to the two celebrities. "Is Mark Richfield going to come back to the show?"

"We're trying. He's a hard one to tempt." Carl raised his eyebrow. "Believe me. There's nothing Keith and I want more."

"Mark who?" Tony looked pinched. Conrad imagined talking about men who had succeeded in Hollywood made him jealous.

Dean replied, "Mark Richfield, the *Dangereux* Cologne model. What rock have you been living under?"

"Me?" Tony pressed his hand to his chest indignantly. "You all sound like a bunch of raving queens."

Conrad bristled in fury but before he could react, Will's voice boomed over an invisible speaker, "I think the toilets need cleaning, Mr. Tony."

"Yeah, so?" Tony looked up at the camera.

"Now."

"What? What did I do?"

"Go." Charlotte urged Tony into the house. "We need a little chat."

Keith blew out an audible breath when Tony was escorted through the sliding doors and they were closed behind him. "Is he the token homophobe?"

Conrad knew Tony's secret. He just wondered if he should blurt it out carelessly without thinking about it first.

"I hope she makes him use his toothbrush." Kelvin pouted.

"Don't be so hard on him," Carl said. "Some guys are more shy than others."

"Shy?" Sonny choked. "Uh. You don't know him."

"Don't we?" Carl grinned.

Conrad suspected they were all gay now. All of them. The pretty boy photo shoot, the openly gay stars. He got it. Hit like a deer in the headlights of a Peterbilt. *Out. They want us to come out. We're all gay and in the closet. How the hell did they know?*

Once Charlotte returned with a red-faced Tony, she huddled their group together to speak to them. "If you want to watch the shoot, you have to be quiet."

Conrad had never seen Charlotte look so serious. Obviously her 'real' work meant a lot to her.

"One peep and you go to your room. Clear?"

"Clear," the five responded, while Tony glared at her, arms tightly knotted over his chest.

"I mean it. Even whispers carry to the camera." She met each of them in the eye before she continued. "That camera has a red light. When it's on, we're recording. I want all of you to sit still. No rustling."

"You sure you want us here?" Tony asked.

"I'm sure I want everyone but you here, Tiger." She grinned.

He shut up.

"Okay. Go move the chaise lounges to that area there." She pointed to the right side of the patio, away from the pool and filming area. "Use three, double up."

Conrad felt like grabbing Sonny to be his partner before anyone else did. The last thing he needed was Kelvin squirming on his lap, or Tony snarling.

Dean and Alfonso dragged a chair each as Tony managed to motivate himself to do something other than complain.

Alfonso signaled silently to Sonny, indicating for him to take the open chair.

Conrad suddenly imagined high-school gym class where the uncoordinated kids were picked last for kickball teams.

"Get your ass over here." Sonny sat on the chaise and waved Conrad over.

"You gotta be kidding." Kelvin did not look pleased he was stuck with Tony as Dean and Alfonso sat together.

"Come here, baby-cakes." Tony sweetened his tone and relaxed on the chaise.

Conrad sat at the very foot of Sonny's chair nervously. Leaning his elbows on his knees he kept his attention on the set up of the filming to come.

The area grew very quiet. Charlotte gave the men a last warning glance before she said, "Let's go," to her crew.

A man with a clapper board said, "Pool scene, take one. Action!"

Conrad's adrenalin dumped. He'd never seen an actual Hollywood taping and felt like he was very privileged indeed. For some reason, he was suffering anxiety for Keith and Carl, like they were under so much pressure he felt sorry for them.

And seeing Charlotte's silent signals to them, Conrad held his breath as the two stars exited the house wearing bathing suits.

"I swear, Troy, getting away for a day was the best thing you ever suggested."

Conrad smiled in pure delight as the actors used their character names. Carl was Troy Wright and Keith was his lover, Dennis Jason, partners both in real life and in the show.

"Alone. Blissfully alone," Carl said, taking a look around him.

"Alone to…?" Keith curled his arm around Carl's waist.

Instantly Conrad's cock pressed against the fabric of his shorts. The steamy love scenes between these two men were on gay internet magazines, YouTube, fan sites, everywhere. And Conrad could not get enough of them.

"To…" Carl embraced Keith tightly.

In a sweeping motion, Carl jumped into the pool and took Keith with him. The splash surprised Conrad and he sat upright.

When the men surfaced they both slapped their soggy bathing suits onto the side of the deck.

Holy shit! Conrad wondered if his heaving breaths were audible to the camera. As the two actors began making out, their perfect physiques visible under the moving water, Conrad went crazy. When he felt a hand on his arm, Conrad nearly shouted and jumped out of his skin. He looked back at Sonny. Sonny was trying to haul him closer.

Before Conrad dared to move in contact with Sonny, he peered at Alfonso. Dean was already resting against his chest and to Conrad's astonishment, Kelvin was reclining on Tony in the same way.

Conrad knew just because there were cameras facing the two stars, that didn't mean they weren't being filmed as well. On the contrary. Every action the six of them did would be recorded from every angle.

Am I doing this? Am I going to snuggle against Sonny? Show my family, my friends, my macho construction buddies I'm a fag?

Feeling his reluctance, Sonny released Conrad's arm.

Keith crooned, "Troy, you get me so hot. I need you in me."

Oh God! Conrad's shorts were growing damp he was so excited.

Carl picked Keith up out of the pool, sitting him on the side and standing between Keith's legs, blocking the camera's view of Keith's cock. Then Carl simulated felatio.

In agony, Conrad rubbed his face and eyes. Sonny's feet shifted soundlessly from the patio to the chair, surrounding Conrad.

"Oh, Troy!" Keith hammed up a coming climax so well, Conrad was about to hump someone.

As Keith went into orgasm-overdrive moaning, Conrad noticed Tony had draped his arms around Kelvin, actually holding him, but not appearing overtly sexual. More as if they were comfortable. Meanwhile, Dean was resting his head on Alfonso's shoulder, looking much more attached to Alfonso than a good friend.

Sonny's legs brushed against Conrad's body. Fingers tickled up and down Conrad's back.

Tears stung Conrad's eyes. He was terrified.

Once Keith had done 'his thing', Carl rolled him over and the act of taking him from behind began.

Ah, Hollywood. No lube? No condom? Yeah, that's Forever Young's style alright. Seeing Carl's ass cheeks tighten and his back muscles twitch as he too simulated a sex act, Conrad was beginning to feel uncomfortable. His dick was bent and trying to engorge completely. He imagined standing and leaving, but couldn't because of the disruption. Maybe reaching into his shorts to straighten it out. No.

"Ahhhfuck! Dennis! I love you!" Carl jammed his hips against Keith who arched his back off the tiled rim around the pool and gave a good yell of pleasure.

Conrad peeked downwards. A stain had formed on his light blue shorts. The minute he was set free he was out of there.

Sonny's hand ran across the nape of Conrad's neck sending erotic chills all over him. Conrad wanted nothing more than to slide back and feel Sonny's cock throb.

"Baby!" Keith rolled to his front and cupped Carl's face.

"Thank you for giving us this day on our own."

"Anything for you, lover. Anything." Carl kissed him.

"Cut!"

Before Charlotte could get a word out, Conrad bolted off the chair and into the house. He jogged up the stairs and closed the door to his room behind him, leaning his head on the door and catching his breath.

Then it dawned on him. Cameras.

Slowly he turned to look. One was looking back from its wall perch. There was nowhere to hide.

"Babe?"

Charlotte's voice sounded concerned.

The lump in Conrad's throat made him terrified.

"Let me in."

Having no choice, Conrad opened the door.

Immediately Charlotte held his hand and sat with him on the bed. "You okay?"

"Yes." He needed to wipe his wet eyes but didn't dare. It would show he was a liar.

"Did the scene embarrass you?"

"No. I watch the show all the time."

"What happened?"

Conrad stared at the camera, cursing it, cursing his choice to come on the show. Furious he had met Sonny on a fake 'reality' series where he couldn't court him, have sex with him, grow into a relationship with him. In all honesty, Conrad knew nothing about Sonny, whether the facts about any of them were the truth and Conrad was really the solo butt of the joke. The trust in him had gone.

"Nothing. I just feel like I need a nap."

Charlotte caressed Conrad's jaw with the tenderness of a mom. She also wiped the tear that had escaped and dropped down Conrad's face. "It's okay."

"No. It's not. Can I be alone? Or am I being punished?" Conrad felt more tears coming and if he didn't run away someone would see them, someone other than Charlotte.

"Of course you're not being punished."

"Thank you." Conrad didn't know how much more he had to hint for her to leave without asking her directly.

"We're here for you. All of us."

"I know."

Charlotte kissed Conrad's cheek and before she left she glanced back over her shoulder, giving him a reassuring smile.

I'm not coming out this way! I'm not!

He waited for her to leave and then headed to the bathroom and splashed his face at the sink.

Sonny didn't know if he should feel rejected or not.

Alfonso, Dean, Kelvin, and even Tony were standing around him, ignoring the two actors who were hidden by a sheet as they dressed and the camera crew disassembled the equipment.

If Charlotte had not taken off after Conrad, Sonny would have.

"Babe." Alfonso rubbed Sonny's back. "It's not you."

Though he nodded, Sonny wasn't as certain. "Are we set up to come out? Is that what this is about?"

"Come out of what?" Tony sneered.

"The closet, you moron." Kelvin rolled his eyes.

"All you fuckers are gay?" Tony acted shocked.

"Will you get the hell away from me?" Dean shoved Tony with a straight arm to his chest.

"I think so, Sonny. Yes. It's a set up to come out." Alfonso appeared to just notice he had his personal microphone on. He yanked it off his shorts and tossed it on the lounge chair behind him. After he did, Dean, Kelvin and Sonny did it as well.

"That's against the rules." Tony pointed a finger at them. "And if you dickheads don't think they can hear every word you say with or without them, you're nuts." He headed to the house. "I'm working out. See you all later."

Keith and Carl, dressed in their sleek cotton outfits stood near the men. "It was very nice meeting you." Keith extended his hand.

"You too." Alfonso took his hand. "It was a thrill."

Sonny and the other two housemates exchanged pleasantries with the two celebs before they left.

With Keith and Carl gone, only the two men who had set up the equipment were remaining to take everything down.

Charlotte rejoined them. Sonny immediately approached her. "Is he okay?"

"Yes." She glanced down. "Where's your mike?"

"Come on, Charlotte." Sonny made a gesture for her to understand, opening his hands.

"Uh uh." She wagged her finger, pointed at the pile of electronics and said, "Now."

Dean drew close enough to whisper into Charlotte's ear. "This show intends to out us publicly. Right?"

"No. Get your mike on."

"You're lying." Alfonso crossed his arms. "You had us check a box, gay or straight." He looked at the other three. "What did you guys check?"

Sonny felt sick. "You expected us to come out on this show when none of us are out to our friends or family? That's cruel."

"Leave." She pointed to the door. "Don't like it? You don't have to stay."

Sonny didn't want to go. It wasn't about being a star or

gaining some kind of notoriety, it was about his housemates and his loyalty.

No one made a move.

"Yeah. Thought so." She pointed. "Microphones."

One by one they picked them up and fastened them to their waistbands.

"Bye." Charlotte left them standing with the cleanup crew.

Sonny made eye contact with Alfonso. He wanted to talk privately about what he was thinking, but Alfonso already knew. Sonny mouthed, 'You coming out?'

'Don't know.' Alfonso peeked at Dean. Dean gave him a sympathetic smile.

Kelvin whimpered.

"Don't worry, babe." Dean caressed Kelvin's hair.

As quiet as he could, Kelvin said, "My parents don't know."

"Join the club." Sonny looked up at the second floor window he knew was Conrad's room.

It was easy for Sonny to be brave in his fireman uniform. Not that horrible to be strong and dissect cadavers for class. But come out on a reality show? Why did it never occur to him this was the whole point? He felt like a moron, not a med student.

Conrad lay on his bed with his hands behind his head, thinking.

"Conrad?"

Hearing Sonny's voice, Conrad grew nervous. "Obviously it's not locked."

The door opened and Sonny poked his head in. "You okay?"

"Yes."

"Can I come in?"

"Of course." Conrad sat up against the headboard.

"Look. I'm sorry. I guess…"

Conrad glanced up at the camera and cringed.

Sonny shut up. "Need a goddamn pen," he muttered.

"Why do you think they don't give us anything to write with?"

Appearing frustrated, Sonny sat on the bed, slouched over his lap and rubbed his face.

Conrad scooted next to him and leaned on his shoulder, his hand cupping the microphone on his clothing. "I'm gay."

Sonny glanced at him, noticed him muting the mike and did the same. "My guess is we all are, and this show is meant to out us."

"Gentlemen?"

They turned to the camera at the sound of Will's voice.

"Take your hands off the sound equipment."

After a deep sigh, Conrad did. "Tony is too."

"I had no doubt."

Conrad pressed his mouth to Sonny's earring. "He got wood when we fought."

Sonny nodded, biting his lip. With his back to the camera, Sonny mouthed slowly, "I want to make love to you."

The admission was agony and ecstasy. Conrad made a face of pain to let Sonny know how he felt.

A debate began in Conrad's head about what would happen if he kissed a man on a reality show. How bad would the fallout be? *Bad.*

"Have to wait." Conrad suspected Will's voice would again warn them to speak up, or something to get their confession on tape.

"I live in Philly."

"Damn. Damn." Conrad balled up his fists. His eyes were

drawn to Conrad's shorts. Clearly visible was the outline of his erect cock. "What's the tattoo say?"

Sonny blinked. "Sorry?"

"The one on your cock," Conrad hissed as quietly as he could.

"How did you see it?" Sonny peeked back at the camera quickly.

"This morning."

"It's a Z."

"Z for Zorro?" Conrad smiled.

"No. Zack."

The smile fell from Conrad's face. "Please don't tell me you're in a relationship."

"Not anymore." Sonny stood up. "Uh, so, I think Alfonso is making something good for dinner tonight."

Seeing the escape tactic easily, Conrad rose to his feet. "Oh? What's on the menu?"

"Something healthy, I'm sure." Sonny was talking loudly, almost as if to mock Will Markham.

They headed to the hall and down the stairs. Sonny stopped Conrad before he made it to the bottom. Outside the men were almost finished clearing up the filming equipment.

"We need to figure out which area does not have a camera."

"Good luck," Conrad replied.

"I will. I'll figure it out." He pressed his lips against Conrad's ear. "I want your cock."

"Oh fuck," Conrad moaned.

"What?" Kelvin stopped in his tracks as he headed outside.

"I missed saying goodbye to Keith O'Leary! My sister will kill me." Conrad made it up as he went along. He didn't even have a sister. "She loves him."

"Charlotte promised we'd get signed photos."

"Oh, thank God!" Conrad wiped his brow and kept walking to the kitchen.

Sonny laughed. "You suck as an actor. Don't quit your day job."

"What day job?" Conrad coughed in a laugh.

Chapter Five

As if they were being punished for their microphone removing incident, the group wasn't given any liquid libations. After dinner they gathered in the lounge, sipping hot tea or decaf coffee.

"Any of you ride?" Tony asked.

"I do." Dean slouched low in his spot on the couch.

Conrad thought it was odd at how much human beings were creatures of habit. It was as if they had all claimed certain places in the rooms. Each room. Here in the lounge, Tony sat on one side of an L-shaped sectional, Kelvin on the other, Alfonso on the lounge chair and ottoman, Dean lying lengthwise on a loveseat, while Sonny and Conrad shared the matching sofa.

The dining room was the same. They had all claimed places for dinner. No one had said a word, it just happened.

"What?" Tony asked, looking bored.

"Twenty-ten Fatboy, Special."

"No!" Tony sat up in his chair. "Which one?"

"Shrine."

"Shut the fuck up!"

Conrad hadn't seen Tony this excited since he sparred with him.

Kelvin asked, "Does anyone know what he's saying?"

"What do you ride?" Dean asked.

"Ninety-five Sportster, 883DLX. Mint. Black and chrome. You been to Sturgis?"

"Never have. You?"

"How could you not have been to Sturgis?" Tony waved Dean off as if he were crazy.

Conrad grinned at Sonny at the conversation. "A bond is born."

"Can someone translate?" Kelvin removed the rubber band from his hair and fluffed out his long blond tresses.

"Translate for the twink." Tony tilted his head to Kelvin.

"Sturgis," Dean said, "is a monster motorcycle event in Sturgis, South Dakota. Complete madness."

"Ya got that right." Tony looked downright proud.

"The school teacher." Alfonso shook his head.

"What? Teachers have to be uptight librarian-type chicks with their hair in buns and a fat ass? Come on."

"That's you all over," Sonny said.

"Don't get all wise-ass on me, med school." Tony pointed his finger at Sonny. "Had one hellavah good time. Dean, you an' me should ride someday." Tony asked, "Where the hell you from again?"

"Phoenix," Dean said.

"Oh. Fuck that. Meet me at Sturgis." Tony laughed. "I ain't riding all the way to Arizona from New York."

Alfonso bristled. "He 'ain't' meeting you anywhere."

Conrad caught Sonny's eye again and nudged him. He mouthed silently, 'Alfonso loves Dean.'

Tony replied to Alfonso, "Why the hell not? Fuck you, Fonzie. Dean can do what he wants. Right, Deano?"

"Whatever you say, Tony." Dean humored him, winking at Alfonso.

"I'm bored!" Kelvin yelled loudly.

"It is getting dull." Sonny yawned.

"I want my BlackBerry," Kelvin said to the camera.

They waited. Will did not reply.

"That doesn't mean he's not watching," Sonny said to the group. "Goodnight, guys."

Conrad perked up. It was nearing eleven and he wanted Sonny to stay with him. Sonny snuck a squeeze of Conrad's fingers and left the room.

"That's it. Jack off and sleep." Kelvin stretched his back.

"What will tomorrow bring?" Alfonso asked, yawning.

"Can't top Keith and Carl. Sorry." Dean stood and walked near Alfonso, reaching out to haul him up.

Conrad heard Alfonso mutter, "Would love to top Keith and Carl."

Dean laughed softly.

As the men left, Conrad studied Tony's reaction. He actually felt sorry for him. He'd alienated himself by his smart-alecky mouth.

When Kelvin cuddled against him, taking Sonny's spot, Conrad leaned backwards to make a gap between them.

"Are you going to bed, Conrad?"

"Uh…" Conrad noticed Tony watching every move they made.

Kelvin licked Conrad's shoulder.

Conrad couldn't get to his feet quickly enough. "Okay, Kelvin, stop being silly. Ha. Ha. You're really funny." Conrad looked directly into the camera. "Ew!" He wiped his shoulder comically. "Go to bed." Conrad ground his jaw and glared at Kelvin.

"'Night." Kelvin slinked off the couch and slithered out of the room, staring back at Conrad seductively.

That left Conrad and Tony alone.

"You seduced the kid?"

"Me?" Conrad choked and faced Tony.

"Pervert." Tony stood.

"First of all, he's twenty-one and I'm twenty-three so how that makes me perverted and Kelvin a kid is beyond me. Second—" Conrad was about to remind Tony and announce to the world, Kelvin was a male and he wasn't 'into' men.

"Jack ass."

"Hang on. Don't start this again."

"Out of all the housemates, I like you the least."

"Welcome to my world." Conrad crossed his arms defensively.

Tony approached him menacingly. "You think you're tough? Mr. Macho-construction-out of worker?"

"Why are you rubbing that in my face? I can't help that the economy went bad for my field. I'll find work. I'm not collecting unemployment. Don't worry."

"Leave the kid alone, ya faggot."

Conrad was stunned at the venom. "Me?" He pointed to his own chest. "How am I gay?"

"You're lusting after every man in this house."

Conrad was dying. He knew the cameras and microphones were catching every word. "Leave me alone. You're insane." Just as he turned his back to Tony, Tony shoved him.

Conrad regained his balance and glared at him. "What's with you? Why do you keep picking fights with me?"

"'Cause I can't stand the sight of you." Tony invaded Conrad's personal space.

"Then you should avoid me. Do me the favor." Conrad nudged Tony backwards, out of his face.

The action set Tony off. He pushed Conrad again, off

balancing him. Conrad recovered and stepped back. Tony attacked him, getting Conrad into a headlock.

Conrad gripped Tony's arms, prying them off, tripping backwards into the sectional sofa. As he hit it, he fell, landing awkwardly with Tony grappling on top of him.

"Get off me, you asshole!" Conrad wrenched Tony's grip away from his neck. When Tony straddled Conrad, pinning him to the couch and ground his cock into Conrad's groin, Conrad tried to push him backwards. "Stop!"

Tony trapped Conrad's head in his hands and went for Conrad's mouth.

Conrad roared in fury and shoved Tony so hard, Tony went flying, overturning the low coffee table and onto the floor.

Wiping his mouth with the back of his hand, Conrad stood over Tony, panting in rage.

Sonny appeared. "What the fuck?"

The crash had roused the rest of the housemates and one by one they showed up, staring into the room.

"He attacked me!" Tony got to his feet slowly. "I was about to go to bed and this pervo tried to kiss me."

Conrad couldn't even defend himself with an answer he was so upset.

"Sure, Tony." Alfonso approached Conrad. "Come on, babe." He held Conrad's hand and led him out of the room. As Conrad walked out, he heard Tony's ranting. "I swear! He did. The guy's been after my ass since we got to this place."

Conrad felt sick to his stomach at the allegations he was desperately trying to avoid.

Numb, Conrad was led up the stairs and to his bedroom by Alfonso. With Sonny, Dean, Kelvin and Alfonso by his side, Conrad inhaled a few times to calm down.

"Want to talk about it?" Dean asked.

A voice from hall yelled, "Why are you all in there with

him? Why is no one out here comforting me? I'm the victim!"

"Shut up, Tony." Sonny slammed the door shut.

Conrad dropped to his bed. "I don't want to talk about it." He covered his face and felt exhausted.

"The bastard provoked you, right?" Alfonso sat beside Conrad and rubbed his back. "You don't have to tell us. We know. He did it yesterday."

"Same shit." Conrad rubbed his eyes with the heels of his palms.

"Okay, baby. Get rest." Alfonso kissed his hair and stood.

Conrad watched them file out of the room, hearing them whispering to Tony in hushed angry tones. Sonny lagged behind.

'Babe,' he mouthed.

Feeling his heart burning, Conrad mouthed back, 'I want you.'

Sonny looked at the camera as if he wanted to tear it down. Obviously conflicted, Sonny hovered by the door, smoothing his hand over his shaven head.

Conrad craved to hold Sonny so much he had found hell. He heard Sonny breathe, "I'm not out. Goddamn it. I'm not out."

Rising to his feet, Conrad stood in front of him, clenching his fists to resist the urge to hold him, kiss him. "That fucker, Tony, is in the closet so deep, I don't know where they found him."

"Under a sewer cover in New York," Sonny whispered.

"He obviously loves it rough, because he gets wood and goes nuts on me." Conrad peeked at the camera, remembered his mike and died. He must have expressed his agony because Sonny touched his arm in comfort. Conrad added for the audience and his family's sake, "But I'm not gay."

"I know. We have nothing to prove, Conrad."

Seeing the warmth in Sonny's brown eyes overwhelmed him. 'Find a place.'

'I fucking will.' Sonny cleared his throat. "Get some rest. See you in the morning."

"Right. Thanks, Sonny." Conrad didn't want him to go.

Once Conrad shut the door to his room and headed to the bathroom to wash up, Will's voice asked him, "You okay, Conrad?"

"Yes." Conrad looked into the camera lens. "Goodnight, Will."

He didn't get a reply. Conrad continued to get ready for bed. Before he shut the light, he picked up his diary video camera and pointed it at his face. "I don't know why Tony did that. But I think having a few days without women is beginning to drive people crazy." Conrad thought about what else he could say to preserve their secrecy. "It's stupid. They keep depriving us of women. What do they expect from us? We're young horny guys in our prime." Sighing loudly, Conrad said, "Maybe they'll bring in a woman soon." He shut the camera and curled into bed, hoping that was enough to convince his family this place was not turning him gay.

Chapter Six

After a shower and shave, Conrad made his bed and took a moment to stare out at the view from his bedroom window. The water in the pool was still as glass and the sun was shining brightly on another cloudless day. Fears of what his friends and family thought of his first few days on *Got Men?* ran through his mind. What were they showing on primetime? What was just for the internet? Which obscure cable network was actually airing twenty-four hour viewing, and when he got out of this place, how would his life change?

He opened the door to his bedroom and bumped into Tony who was exiting his room, directly opposite Conrad's.

Conrad avoided connecting to his eyes and headed down the stairs hearing the patter of Tony's bare feet behind him. The best way for he and Tony not to fight was to not engage him in conversation. How Conrad was going to do that was yet to be decided.

"Good morning." Alfonso was sorting through a cardboard carton that was on the kitchen counter.

"Our morning delivery?" Conrad asked. "I'd kill for a newspaper."

Tony snickered and poured himself a cup of coffee.

Before either he or Alfonso replied, Sonny grabbed Conrad's arm and dragged him down the hall. Conrad looked back at the other two men who watched curiously.

Sonny pressed his mouth to Conrad's ear. "The laundry room."

"No."

Sonny nodded and walked briskly down the hall. Across from the gym were two doors that were accessed from the hallway. One had a small space with a washer and dryer, the other was locked and no one knew what was behind it.

Looking right, then left, Sonny opened the laundry room door and dragged Conrad in.

Stumbling for balance, Conrad was about to say that their movements would be tracked to the room when Sonny held his finger to his lips and pointed to a camera.

"I thought you said—"

"One." Sonny tilted his head to it and walked directly under its prying lens. He used sign language to point out the view that the one camera had of the small closet-like room.

Conrad stood beside him and inspected the rest of the area. Just to be sure, he hoisted himself up on the dryer and felt around the top of the molding. Hopping down, Conrad nodded in agreement.

They left the room. Sonny said, "See, I told you it was a laundry room," to cover their act.

The excitement Conrad felt at the potential of he and Sonny getting into something physical had him reeling. Being pent up sexually was new to Conrad. He had a boyfriend, an *ex-boyfriend*, he reminded himself, before he came on the show. So sex was frequent. This new level of abstinence was frustrating all of them.

Kelvin witnessed them coming out of the laundry room. "Did you guys get a chore already?"

"No. Not yet." Sonny led the way to the kitchen.

"I just didn't know where the washer/dryer was."

"You would if you got stuck doing the laundry." Kelvin made a sour face.

As Conrad rounded the corner into the kitchen, Dean, Tony and Alfonso were sitting at the dining room table with bowls of cereal in front of them.

"Off the hook, Alfonso?" Conrad asked.

"They only gave us granola and yoghurt. I'd whip something up if I could."

Handing a bowl to Sonny and Kelvin first, Conrad waited as they filled their dish with cereal and milk.

"This sucks." Kelvin joined the men at the table. "I want something greasy, like bacon and sausages. Or hash-browns smothered in cheese and sour cream."

"Yech!" Dean wrinkled his nose. "Sour cream on hash-browns?"

Sonny pulled out the chair beside him for Conrad.

"Thanks," Conrad said. Once they were all together, Conrad asked, "Anyone know the day's events?"

"Not yet." Alfonso drank the remaining milk from his bowl.

"What time is it?" Tony looked around the room.

"Nine." Dean checked his watch.

"Hello, boys!" Charlotte seemed to materialize from thin air.

Conrad jumped out of his skin at hearing her voice behind his back.

"Did you all sleep well?" She made the rounds at the table, patting each man on the head as if they were her beloved pets. "Are the sheets a mess? Do we need to change them?"

"Ha ha." Kelvin finished his granola, pouting.

"I think we're okay, Charlotte." Alfonso chuckled.

"Too bad. Will and I are hoping for messy sheets. Oh, well, there's still so much time."

Conrad couldn't believe the way her eyes lit up at the potential of any of them getting dirty together. "Don't you witness enough sex on your nighttime drama? My God, Charlotte, how much fornication must you watch to be happy?"

"Are you talking about *Forever Young*?" She widened her eyes like a child. "Oh, sweetie, that's all fake. Sorry, but there's no real sex on that show. Did you not know that?"

"If you want us to have sex, why don't you bring us some women?" Conrad figured he throw it out there.

Dean stifled a choke in his throat.

"Women? Will that make you boys happy?" She took his dare.

Now Conrad felt like an idiot. Knowing they were all gay, having women flaunting themselves around them would only prove the point. The last thing Conrad intended on doing was trying to have sex with a woman.

"He's joking, Charlotte." Alfonso gave Conrad an admonishing eye.

"No. No. Perhaps we can get Conrad a woman." Charlotte touched her lip. "Perfect. I'll have your date all lined up for you tonight."

Sonny kicked Conrad under the table. It was all Conrad could do to not react to the pain.

"And I thought this was going to be a boring day." Charlotte's sarcasm was palpable. "Did you bring a nice outfit, Conrad? We can make sure you have dress clothing for your date."

"Date? Like in, out?"

"Of course. Women need to be wined and dined."

Conrad caught Sonny's 'I'm going to kill you' scowl. "That's not necessary, Charlotte."

"Nonsense. Alfonso, no need to make dinner for six tonight. Just five."

His body tensing in fury, Conrad was about to scream. "No, really. I'm not interested in leaving the guys behind."

"See you later, Conrad! Make the most of it. She may be your last woman for the rest of your stay here." Charlotte waved and Conrad could hear her laughter as she left the house.

Sonny stood, threw his bowl into the sink with a smash and left the room.

Will's voice echoed in the house, "Sonny has clean up duty in the kitchen."

Tony's sneering smirk made Conrad want to punch him. "Nice one, Conny. Don't worry. We'll keep Sonny busy."

Kelvin glared at Conrad as well. "I hate you."

"What?" Conrad waved his hands. "Guys…"

Rising up, pushing out his chair, Kelvin left the room in a huff.

Still laughing about it, Tony placed his and Kelvin's dishes in the sink and vanished.

Conrad was left with Alfonso and Dean, staring at him from across the table.

"How badly do you need to prove your manhood?" Alfonso asked.

"Bad enough to hurt Sonny?" Dean leaned towards Conrad.

Paranoid of the cameras rolling, not to mention the microphones, Conrad said again, "Come on, guys."

"Have a nice date." Dean set his and Alfonso's bowl in the sink and walked out of the room.

Numb, feeling like the biggest ass on the planet, Conrad stared into space for a long time, hearing the others chatting, the treadmill in the gym beginning to move, and doors opening and closing. It took an effort but Conrad stood, moved to the sink and began cleaning up the chards of ceramic from Sonny's broken bowl.

"Sonny is assigned kitchen duty," Will reminded him.

"Tough." Conrad got rid of the broken dish and washed up, using a sponge to wipe the counters. Once the room was in order, Conrad did a walk through to see where everyone was. Sonny and Kelvin were in the gym and the other three were lounging by the pool.

Through the whirr of the treadmill noise, and Kelvin's heavy footfalls, Conrad approached Sonny who was lying face up on the bench under a loaded bar.

He crouched down next to him. "You know why I did it."

"Yup." Sonny didn't make eye contact and worked his palms on the bar.

"When can we meet in the laundry room?" He peeked back at Kelvin who was ignoring him.

"Don't know."

"Sonny…" Conrad wanted to stroke his cheek.

"I'm busy." Sonny hefted the bar off the rack to his chest.

"I can spot."

"Don't need one."

Hurt, Conrad backed up and watched Sonny as he did his bench press repetitions. Head down, Conrad met with the other men outside.

"Get lost, ya piranha." Tony sneered.

"What?" Conrad threw up his hands. "Because I said we should see a woman?" He looked directly at Alfonso. "Even you don't understand what I'm doing?"

"We get it, Conrad." Alfonso appeared as hurt as Sonny.

Sitting down on Alfonso's lounge chair, Conrad tried to speak softly but he knew everything was heard. "Please understand."

"We all do." Alfonso met his eyes. "You do what you have to do, babe."

"Then why are you all making me feel so shitty about it?"

“Are we? Or are you doing it to yourself?” Dean asked.

“Moron,” Tony muttered under his breath.

If Conrad didn’t think Tony was right, he would have egged him on for battle. But this time, the Tiger from the Bronx had it dead on.

While the others chatted about their lives in the ‘real’ world, Conrad kept watch through the back window into the gym. After a half hour, Sonny replaced the weights onto the rack and walked to the hall.

Conrad leapt to his feet and entered the house, blocking Sonny’s path up the stairs to his room.

“What?” It appeared Sonny’s workout did not relieve his anger.

“Laundry time.” Conrad gripped Sonny’s arm.

“No, man,” Sonny hissed through his teeth. “Not in daylight.”

“You think they don’t have night-vision cameras?” Conrad lowered his voice and leaned with one hand on the wall in front of Sonny. “I have to make it up to you.”

“Break the date.” Sonny crossed his arms.

Conrad looked for a camera, found one in the hall and yelled, “I’m not going out tonight, Will.”

“I’m afraid you are.”

“No.” Conrad waited for another reply. None came.

Sonny moved out of the tight space Conrad created and headed up the stairs.

Conrad showed his teeth at the camera lens. “No!”

“Any reason why not, Conrad?” Will’s voice sounded so amused Conrad wanted to puke. “If it’s a good reason, I’ll think about it.”

He knew what Will wanted. He wasn’t ready to give it to him. “I’m tired! I don’t want to go out. I just want to relax.”

Will made a buzzing sound. “Nope. Not good enough.”

"Will!"

Kelvin nudged Conrad harshly from behind. "Excuse me. I have to shower."

"Geez." Conrad watched Kelvin trudge up the stairs. "I didn't do anything!" Conrad yelled after Kelvin. But he knew he had. He betrayed everyone.

How five men confined to an eleven room house managed to avoid him all day was beyond Conrad's comprehension. If he entered the kitchen, the rest regrouped in the lounge; if he relaxed in the lounge, they scampered out to the patio. Finally getting the obvious hint, Conrad stayed in his room, lying on his bed, brooding.

Five o'clock a light tap brushed the door. Hoping it was Sonny, Conrad called, "Come in."

Charlotte entered. "You're not ready. Go get changed."

"I'm not going."

"I'm afraid you are." She walked to his closet and he could hear the hangers sliding.

Conrad didn't budge.

A pair of black slacks and a cotton shirt was thrown on him. "If you don't change, I'll get my goons to dress you."

Enraged, but really mad at himself, Conrad stood and yanked his gym shorts down, stepping into the trouser legs.

"A limousine is out front." She handed him black socks and his leather shoes.

"Goody." Once he'd put them on, Conrad reached for the shirt and buttoned the front. As he tucked in his shirttails Charlotte fussed with his hair. "Needs a brushing."

He stormed into the bathroom and ran his brush over his head. While he did, Charlotte uncapped a bottle of cologne and dabbed it on his neck.

He sniffed it. It wasn't his. "Where'd you get that?"

"*Dangereux* Cologne. Sure to drive women mad."

"Whatever."

"You can still get out of this." She met his eyes in the mirror's refection as she clamped his microphone to his shirt.

"I'm not doing what you want me to do." His mouth formed a tight line.

"Have a nice night." She waved eloquently, sending him on his way.

When Conrad made it to the front hall, the group was drinking booze in the lounge, staring at him. Conrad caught Sonny's eyes. The fury Conrad was feeling was only matched by the night he and his ex broke up. If he didn't leave the house now, he'd put a hole through the plasterboard wall.

He nearly broke the hinge on the door going outside.

"My!" Charlotte laughed. "Aren't you thrilled we got you a date with a woman and out of the house? You may want to tell the viewers why when we grant your wish you're full of spite."

"Be quiet." He waited as the chauffeur opened the back door.

"Bye, sweetie!" Charlotte threw him a kiss.

The minute the limousine door was shut Conrad spotted two cameras pointed at him, one on each of the front seat headrests.

Fucking sons of bitches. They know what they're doing to me. He felt throbbing in his temples. *What I did to myself!*

In a zone of daydreaming and imagining sucking Sonny's cock, Conrad felt the car stop and tried to see out of the tinted window. The back door opened and long legs in a micro-mini skirt with spiked stiletto heels appeared. The woman ducked into the back seat with him and smiled. "Hello."

Conrad jolted at her appearance. Not only was she gorgeous, he felt chills wash over him that she may not be completely female. And that scared the shit out of him.

"Hi." He held out his hand for a shake.

"I'm Trinity." She sat next to him, crossing her legs causing her skirt to ride up even higher.

"I'm Conrad." It came out like a croak he was so nervous.

"I know who you are, honey."

God! She's a he! She's a he! What are they doing to me?

Trinity rubbed Conrad's thigh assertively as the car moved on. "Charlotte tells me you're starved for female attention. Well, pretty man. Here I am."

Oh, God! Conrad glanced at her abundant cleavage. *Pre-op? Post-op? Those are boobs not falsies. Her hair was not a wig. It was jet black and thick and shining. Her lashes were real as well, dark, framing her expertly painted blue eyes.*

If he were a dumb jock from the mid-west, he'd have no clue she was not a real she. But Conrad had seen enough trannies to know one when he met one. This one was good. Damn good. Almost good enough to fool him. *She was a he, right?* He began to get second thoughts. He inspected all the signs that would give her away. Adam's apple, hands, any face stubble. No. Is this a woman?

"Conrad?"

"Huh?" He woke up.

"I know you've been living in a house full of men and want a woman's attention." Her hand crept closer to his balls.

He tensed up and pressed back into the seat.

"Baby…let me satisfy you." She cupped his crotch and licked his earlobe.

Cameras. Cameras! Everywhere. Okay. If I push her away am I confirming I'm gay? If I kiss her, am I really going to kiss a transsexual? Am I? I want to kiss Sonny. Not Trinity. Trinity? What kind of name is Trinity? It's a gay man's name for a woman-persona. I don't believe this.

"Ahh!" Conrad gasped as she poked her finger up his

bottom through his pants. *You're a man. A woman wouldn't do that. You're a man!* He cleared his throat. "Aren't we going to dinner?"

"I know what I want for my appetizer." She popped open the top of his trousers.

Through his teeth Conrad whispered, "Did they tell you to do this?"

"Honey, you are too hot to keep my hands off of. Rowr!"

Conrad stared at the back of the chauffeur's head as Trinity dug in his pants for his dick. What would a straight guy do? *Would he let this she/he suck him off? Why me?*

"I…I don't want to do this in a car with cameras watching me, Trinity." Conrad tried to close his zipper.

She pouted out her lower lip like a B-movie actress. "Charlotte said I was here to give you release. Would you rather make love?" She dragged her skirt up and Conrad faced the window quickly.

"No. How about a nice dinner?" He closed his pants.

She climbed on top of Conrad's lap and straddled his thighs.

Before Conrad could protest, Trinity pushed his head from behind and he had him drowning in cleavage. As she rubbed her breasts all over him, Conrad closed his eyes and didn't know how much he could take. "No. Uh, thanks though." He held Trinity's shoulders and made a gap between them so he could both breathe and see her eyes. Conrad mouthed, 'Don't do this to me.'

Digging her hands into his hair, Trinity drew Conrad to her lips. When they connected, her tongue darted into his mouth. Conrad pushed her back more forcefully. "Please! I said no. Can't we just go eat somewhere?"

"You don't want me?" She gave him that imitation pout again.

"I don't know you." Conrad knew this was going to kill his

reputation, no matter what he did.

"You don't have to know me." She grabbed his nuts and kissed his neck.

"What do I have to do to get you to stop?" he whispered into her ear.

"They paid me too much, honey. Sorry."

God no! Conrad was an emotional train wreck. He used more strength than he would with a woman, and set Trinity on the seat next to him. "Sorry, babe. You're not my type."

"Whatever! Don't whine for pussy if you don't really want it, Conrad." She fluffed up her hair and tapped the divider. The driver lowered it. "Take me home. Our boy here doesn't want to play. He's just pretending to want a real girl."

"Real girl?" Conrad choked and got a fiery look from Trinity.

"Want to clarify that?" She looked like she may murder him.

"No." Conrad slouched down low and pressed his face to the window. "Just shoot me."

"Gotta gun?"

Conrad glanced at her angry expression and kept quiet.

Sonny paced. He'd already had too much to drink and no one could calm him down. If he said what was really on his mind, he would be out. Out! That's the name of the game. Not *Got Men? Get Men Out*!

Needing to be alone, Sonny stood near the pool and tried to see the stars. It was only seven but a few were beginning to glow in the heavens. He wished he'd never taken time off of work and school. He thought he needed the break because the stress of everything back in Philly was getting too heavy. And when he broke up with Zack…

Sonny rubbed his face tiredly. That was the topper. So he

answered an ad in the paper for a reality show. He expected to put up with snakes, spiders, evictions, loose women, not this. Not being forced to do something he was not ready for.

After med school, after he interned, after he set up his own practice or got a job at a hospital. Not now.

And that didn't even begin to explain what his tough macho fire-fighting co-workers would say to him. The teasing would be merciless.

His family was devout Baptist. *No. I can't come out on national TV and international Internet. That would be insane.*

So? What was he supposed to do about Conrad?

Sonny sat on the foot of the chaise lounge and lost his focus on the lights in the pool.

The minute he laid eyes on that big, buff blond he was smitten. The guy was everything Sonny liked. Light eyes, over six feet tall, powerful, masculine…

And Conrad was hot for him.

If they had met in a club, the sex would be amazing. But instead, Conrad was so petrified of the gay label, he was pretending to be the tough straight jock. He didn't fool any of the housemates. Was he fooling the audience?

Sonny had no clue what scenes, what dialogue or what hours were aired on prime time, but he knew how these things went. It would be the steamiest, the most controversial or the most violent. That's what the viewers craved and what Will Markham and Derek Dixon were famous for.

"Hey."

Sonny spun back to the door. Conrad was standing there.

He checked his watch. "Forty minutes? That was your big date?"

Conrad sat down next to Sonny on the lounge and leaned against his shoulder. "Didn't even eat. All we did was drive around aimlessly."

"Oh? Nice blowjob though?" Sonny wanted to be mad, but he knew Conrad's motivation and felt sorry for him.

"Uh no." Conrad rustled his hand over his mike to disguise the conversation. "They set me up with a post-op."

"No!" Sonny covered his smile.

"She was good," Conrad nodded, his eyes wide.

"You let her suck your dick?" Sonny almost rose up.

"No!" Conrad held him down. "She was a good tranny. I didn't let her do a fucking thing to me." Conrad cupped his hand over the mike. "She tried and she failed."

"How did you get out of it?" Sonny rustled his mike as well. "After asking for sex with a woman?"

"I didn't ask for sex!" Conrad appeared exasperated. "I didn't say I wanted sex with a woman. Sheesh. You know exactly what I said and why."

"Who do you want sex with?" Sonny purred.

Conrad took a paranoid look at the back patio's plethora of cameras. As he did, he rubbed his own crotch.

"Laundry room. Tonight." Sonny bit his lip, eying the prying camera lenses.

"Time?"

"Midnight."

"Deal."

As they both entered the house again, Conrad felt as if he owed the men his apology. Standing on the threshold of the lounge, seeing plenty of empty beer bottles and shot glasses littering the coffee and side tables, Conrad knew the housemates were feeling no pain.

"I'm sorry."

Alfonso replied, "No need to apologize, babe."

"Yes. I did need to."

"Get your pussy fix?" Tony asked, not looking at Conrad.

"That's my business." Conrad shook his head at the other three and mouthed, 'No.'

Kelvin brightened up. "Look at you. All dressed up."

Looking down at his attire, Conrad said, "I feel better in a pair of shorts."

Dean asked, "Why did you come back so quickly? Did you head to a drive-thru fast food joint?"

"Didn't even get to eat. I'm starving." Conrad felt Sonny standing beside him. "How was dinner here?"

"Good." Sonny gave him an affectionate grin.

"Anything left?"

"Nope." Tony finally turned his head in Conrad's direction. "I ate all of it."

"We didn't know you'd not get a chance to eat," Alfonso said, "Want me to see what I can do?"

"Is there granola left?"

"I think so." Kelvin sat up. "Want me to check?"

"I got it. Thanks, though."

"Why are you guys being so nice to the asshole?" Tony thumbed over his shoulder in Conrad's direction.

"We like him." Kelvin smiled.

"Yeah. We like him." Sonny squeezed Conrad's shoulder.

"Thanks, guys." Conrad felt so much better as he headed to the kitchen for a snack. While he removed the box of granola from the cupboard, Sonny took the milk out of the refrigerator.

Kelvin joined them, sitting on a stool at the counter. "What was she like?"

Conrad mouthed, 'Post-op tranny.'

"Huh?" Kelvin appeared confused.

Dean, who had caught it as he and Alfonso entered the room, leaned to Kelvin's ear to whisper into it.

"Oh!" Kelvin's eyes went wide. "Are you kidding me?"

"No." Conrad climbed onto a stool and ate his cereal.

"That's unreal. But sooo Charlotte!" Alfonso shook his head. "Pretty one at least?"

"Fucking gorgeous. If I was a hick I never would have known."

"What the fuck are you then?" Tony leaned against the counter.

"Go away!" Conrad moaned.

Sonny stood behind Conrad and massaged his shoulders. "Glad it wasn't me."

"They had cameras in the back of the car." Conrad knew they were being taped right now, but didn't give a shit about this topic being aired. "She attacked me." He laughed, pouring more milk into his bowl.

"How?" Kelvin leaned his chin in his palm.

"Grabbed my nuts, sat on my lap…" Conrad finished the last bite and nudged the bowl away.

Alfonso took it to the sink to wash.

"I'll do it."

"I got it." Alfonso placed it into the rack after he rinsed it.

"What did she look like?" Dean sat next to Conrad at the counter.

"Petite, jet black hair, blue eyes." Conrad held his hands in front of his chest. "Big implants."

"Son of a bitch!" Dean shook his head. "Like, really convincing?"

"Yes. I kept going back in forth in my head if I was right or wrong. I know I was right."

"Weaves?" Alfonso asked.

"No. Her own hair. Nice too."

"Was she ethnic? You know, Asian or something?" Kelvin

looked fascinated.

“Maybe. Not something overt, but possibly part Filipino or something. But we’re talking totally American born.”

Sonny dug his fingers into Conrad’s hair, getting amorous. It began to make Conrad paranoid again. “Hey. That tickles.” He swatted Sonny’s hand away playfully.

Sonny backed away, appearing slightly insulted. Conrad gave him an imploring look.

“Don’t ask for a woman again, guys.” Alfonso put away the milk and cereal. “Big trouble.”

“Lesson learned.” Conrad laughed.

“Would you have fucked her if she was a real woman, Conny?”

Conrad met Tony’s eyes. He knew that comment was meant for the cameras.

“I don’t make love to anyone I just met.” Conrad leaned both his elbows on the table.

“Bullshit!” Tony choked. “You tellin’ me you never had a one night stand? Never?”

“No.” Conrad tried to ignore him, about to change the subject and ask Alfonso what he had prepared for dinner.

“You know how many women I fucked one time?” Tony said.

“Who cares?” Kelvin rolled his eyes.

“He does.” Dean tilted his head to Tony.

“Listen, douche bags, I was married once. I’m not a fag like the rest of you.”

Conrad stood off the chair and puffed up in anger. “Want me to tell them, tough guy?”

“Tell em what?” Tony echoed the body language.

“Uh, guys… Not again.” Dean held out his hands.

“Tell them…” Conrad wanted to. Wanted to describe the

kissing and humping, but outting a man against his will was not in his nature. He wouldn't want anyone doing it to him.

"Tell em what?" Tony threw up his hands. "Come on, Conny. Tell em that you hump me every time we fight? That you fucking tried to kiss me?"

Conrad nudged Tony out of his way as he stormed out of the room.

"Don't you push me and run away, pussy!" Tony yelled.

Conrad threw open his bedroom door and grabbed the diary camera, turning it on and pointing it at his face. "Will, if you don't get him away from me, I'm going to kill him."

Chapter Seven

Conrad lay awake in bed.

Thinking about Sonny and their planned meeting, Conrad wondered how they would sneak past infrared night cameras, both enter the laundry room at midnight, and come out together after. Or even one at a time. How do you explain that? Midnight laundry? Stain pre-scrubbing? Ironing while sleep-walking?

No. Even if their actual sex act could not be seen, the image of their clandestine meeting would be. They could not escape the ubiquitous cameras, day or night.

Did that mean he would stand Sonny up? Hell no!

How could they do it? Even if he hid his face with a shirt, the camera would catch which bedroom doors men exited from. Planning this all night, Conrad had left his door wide open so at least the sight of it moving wouldn't be a problem.

He had to touch Sonny. He couldn't take wanting him and not being able to kiss him.

Using his two pillows, Conrad pushed them under the blankets lengthwise so they created a lump in the bed.

He took a peek at the camera, judging its angles again. As quickly as he could he rolled off mattress and edged under the bed. On his belly he inched to the open door. Though it was pitch dark in his room, he knew this was crazy. The night vision lenses would catch him. It didn't matter. He could say he and

Sonny had a long heart to heart talk. If no one saw them having sex, no one would really know for certain.

Conrad kept to the walls as he walked to the staircase which was just outside his room. Holding his breath, he tiptoed down the slatted stairs and paused. He jiggled a door handle. It was locked. Suddenly he realized he was at the wrong door. Scooting to the next, he opened it and entered. He was there first.

The camera had a blinking red light indicating it was recording everything. He cursed it and opened the dryer as if he was doing laundry. Something no one would buy since he never turned on a light.

Hearing a tiny noise, Conrad inched to the far wall, under the camera's view, and waited.

Sonny slipped in, closed the door soundlessly and sprinted towards him.

"You know the cameras in the hall witnessed everything."

"You want to abort the plan?" Sonny touched Conrad's chest.

"Fuck no." He rested his hand behind Sonny's head and drew him to his lips. On contact, Conrad felt an explosion in his groin.

It had all the desperation of two men who had been starved for a lifetime and had finally gotten to eat.

Conrad opened his mouth to Sonny's tongue and wanted to whimper in relief so much he actually had to consciously shut up.

Sonny slipped his hand down the front of Conrad's shorts. When that hot palm wrapped around his dick, Conrad spread his legs and gripped Sonny so tightly by his shoulders he was stunned Sonny didn't cry out from the pain.

Gasping for air between kisses, Conrad was lost on Sonny's soft lips and dexterous tongue. If it were up to Conrad, he'd kiss him all night, but they had to be quick. Air surrounded

Conrad's dick. He looked down to see it exposed from his shorts, stiff as a rod.

Though he wanted to speak, tell Sonny how incredible it was, Conrad said nothing and forced himself not to pant like an overheated St Bernard. Sonny licked down Conrad's neck to his chest. With his cock being pumped and squeezed, his nipples chewed, Conrad was on the edge already.

Smoothing his hands over Sonny's head, neck, shoulders and muscular back, Conrad couldn't wait for his turn at playing with him. A hot tongue drew a line down his midsection to his cock.

Conrad tensed his body as his cock sank into Sonny's sucking mouth. "Holy crap," he whispered as softly as he could.

His balls were flipped out of his shorts and groped, massaged, tugged on. The minute Sonny impaled his ass with a wet finger, Conrad came. His knees gave out and he pressed his back against the wall to stay upright. Sealing his lips so he wouldn't grunt like a rutting sow, Conrad felt his balls tighten to a knot and a surge of cum went through his length.

Sonny gave him a little whimper of delight as he swallowed.

The only light, ironically, was from the blinking red bulb on the overhead camera. But Conrad didn't mind using his sense of touch, taste, smell and hearing to enjoy this beauty.

The moment he could function, Conrad held Sonny as close as he could to his chest and swapped spots. He kissed Sonny's lips, tasting his own cum and then used big wet licks down Sonny's throat to his nipple. With his teeth he tugged on the erect tip and craved sucking and playing with Sonny all night. Soon. After they left the show. Not now. Not here.

He kissed and chewed his way down Sonny's body, feeling every rippling muscle under Sonny's taut skin. Conrad inhaled deeply and felt his mouth water at the scent of a man and musky soap. With both his hands in Sonny's waistband, Conrad yanked down his gym shorts and felt Sonny's cock slap him under the chin. He grabbed it in one hand and tried to fit the whole thing into his mouth. Sonny gripped Conrad's hair in response, so Conrad knew it was intense for him as well. He fondled Sonny's low hanging sack and pulled and maneuvered the balls inside, rubbing the root with hot friction.

A taste of pre-cum followed and Conrad wanted the mother-load. He deep-throated Sonny until his nose was in his dark, curly pubic hair. After feeling that cock pulsate on his tongue, Conrad began drawing to the tip with strong pulling suction imagining sucking that tattooed Z off and replacing it with a C. He stuck his index finger into his mouth quickly to wet it, and pushed inside Sonny's ass, massaging his prostate. A deep throbbing contraction preceded Conrad's mouth filling with spunk.

Both of Sonny's hands tugged Conrad's hair and as he pulled on it, he fucked Conrad's mouth until he stopped coming.

Conrad was in love—madly, out of this world love. Sex with this man was so good it made the contact with his cold-ex partner wane into extinction.

Conrad made sure he milked every drop, then kissed his way back up to Sonny's mouth. Sonny hugged him with so much force, Conrad couldn't breathe deeply. The frenzied kissing was making Conrad dizzy. He cupped Sonny's face in both hands and between their lips he hissed as quietly as he could, "You're fantastic! I loved it! Jesus Christ!"

"Babe…oh my God. Babe!" Sonny humped him wildly.

"I don't want to stop." Conrad held their two cocks together and felt them come to life again.

"We can't. Babe. At least we know. We know."

"Yes." Conrad shut up and peeked over his head at the red light. "You want to go first?"

"I'll head to the kitchen and get a glass of water."

"If they confront us, tell them we wanted a private chat

about my horrible night."

"Yes. Good. Perfect."

"You are perfect." Conrad held Sonny's jaw and kissed him again.

Sonny took a last squeeze of Conrad's cock and balls and nodded he was ready. As Conrad pressed his back against the wall, Sonny darted out of the room.

Flipping his cock back into his shorts, Conrad couldn't believe he had met a man as incredible as Sonny. If nothing else, this crazy reality show did that for him.

Counting to twenty, Conrad flew out of the room and towards the stairs, headlong into someone. He gasped and nearly fell, reaching out to catch whomever it was he had body slammed in the dark.

Sloshing of liquid got him wet and he dreaded the fact that he had met with Sonny, but this was not Sonny. Judging by his size, it had to be Kelvin.

"Where did you come from?" Kelvin gasped.

"Uh. I was thirsty too."

"So you were running to get a drink in the wrong direction? That's nuts."

Conrad couldn't justify an answer to that question.

"Sonny's in the kitchen."

"Is he?" Conrad headed to the stairs.

"Where are you going now?"

"I changed my mind." Conrad climbed the slats to the upper floor. When he felt Kelvin touching his ass, he whispered, "Don't do that. I'll trip."

"You are so handsome, Conrad."

"Thanks, Kelvin." Conrad did not need this at the moment. He assumed Kelvin was a good boy and had his microphone on.

"Like really handsome."

"Thanks." Conrad stood at his door. "Goodnight, Kelvin. See you in the morning."

"Goodnight, Conrad."

Was there any point acting like James Bond and belly crawling into his room now? Kelvin and he were obviously filmed coming up the stairs and into the hall.

Conrad walked directly to his bathroom and turned on the light. The liquid he was covered with was orange juice. He tightened his mouth to a frown and took a washcloth to his chest to clean up.

"Sticky, Conrad?"

A cold chill passed over Conrad's back causing the hair to rise on his neck. "Go to sleep, Will."

"I could say the same to you. Sweet dreams, Conrad."

Shutting the light, Conrad knew the jig was up. He crawled into bed and fixed his pillows, trying not to worry about it so much that he couldn't sleep.

Chapter Eight

The scent of coffee and food instantly hit Conrad's senses when he began his trek to the first floor. Hearing Alfonso and Dean's voices, he wondered if one of them set a clock alarm and that was how they managed to get up first all the time.

When Conrad rounded the bend to be able to see them, they were rubbing shoulders, giving each other seductive smiles and whispering.

Conrad cleared his throat and approached a counter with mugs for coffee.

"Hi, Conrad." Dean appeared as if he were delirious.

"Hello," Conrad replied, smiling but curious.

"Crepes this morning." Alfonso gave Conrad the same wicked grin Dean had.

A feeling of anxiety hit Conrad. They all knew about him and Sonny? Already? Was there a newsletter slipped under the door written by someone on Will's team that was brought with the morning food allocation?

Conrad sipped his coffee and drew near the two men. "You guys…uh…"

"Uh…" Dean's grin was unnerving Conrad.

"You know." Conrad made useless gestures with his free hand.

"Uh huh." Dean was glowing. "Oh yeah."

"Look. I have no idea how you know—"

"How we know?" Alfonso laughed softly as he whisked the batter.

Conrad shut up. He was confused.

"What are you talking about?" Dean asked.

"Morning!" Kelvin appeared chipper. "Please don't tell me we're having rabbit food granola again."

Conrad began going crazy at what he didn't know about Dean and Alfonso.

"Nope, baby. Crepes." Alfonso began pouring the thin batter into a pan.

"Crepes?" Kelvin hunched over his coffee at the counter. "No bacon and homefries yet?"

Dean smiled sweetly at him. "There's still time. Maybe Mr. Markham will indulge you soon."

"Hey." Sonny went for the coffee pot, taking the last of it and rinsing it to make more.

"Morning, Sonny." Dean had the same devilish smirk on his lips as when he said good morning to Conrad. It was driving Conrad nuts.

"Anyone find a pen anywhere?" Conrad began opening drawers.

"They don't want us to write, babe." Alfonso flipped the crepe.

"Why is the coffee pot always empty when I get here?" Tony groaned.

"I'm making a fresh pot. Have mine. I just poured it." Sonny pointed to his cup.

"I don't want yours."

"Then be quiet." Sonny continued scooping out grounds.

"Be careful," Kelvin said, "Or you'll get kitchen duty."

Tony leaned over Alfonso's shoulder. "What the hell is that? More girlie food?"

"Make your own." Dean didn't sound angry. He sounded apathetic.

Conrad was about to scream at Alfonso, 'Do you know what me and Sonny did last night?'

Obviously changing his mind, Tony took possession of Sonny's cup and added milk. Once he was propped up on a stool next to Kelvin he said, "Did you sleep well, babydoll?"

"Got thirsty. There was like a convention going on down here at midnight." Kelvin laughed.

Immediately Alfonso and Dean spun around to Kelvin. "Convention?" Dean asked.

Maybe they don't know. Conrad was beyond confused.

"What did you all do last night?" Tony asked. "Late swim or something?"

Sonny peered at Conrad sheepishly.

"No. I think Kelvin is overstating it. He just got himself a glass of juice." Conrad caught Dean's eye. Now Dean looked as befuddled as he did.

"No, I'm not overstating anything." Kelvin laughed. "Sonny was down here and so were you."

Conrad's face went hot and Sonny sank against the counter, saying, "Kelvin, there're no rule about getting a drink."

"I never said there was."

Tony appeared pinched. Enraged. His usual.

Dean mouthed to Conrad, 'Did you and Sonny?'

Glancing at Tony first, seeing him catching everything, Conrad took his coffee and left the room. "Call me when it's done, Alfonso."

"Will do, champ."

Walking to the back of the house, Conrad stood at the glass slider to check on the pool.

Feeling warmth mingle with his own, Conrad peeked over his shoulder at Dean. Dean leaned close to Conrad's ear to whisper, "I slept with Alfonso last night."

Choking mid-sip, Conrad sprayed the glass with coffee and coughed, trying not to spill the remainder in his cup.

"Wow." Dean gave Conrad a look of disbelief and left, returning with a dishtowel to wipe the door. "You okay?"

With a purposeful expression of exaggeration, Conrad allowed his jaw to drop. He mouthed, 'You're out?'

"I suppose." Dean shrugged, swiping at the sliding door.

Conrad glanced down the hall, then at their microphones, and at the camera watching them. He opened the slider and dragged Dean with him near the pool. After setting his cup down on a table, Conrad took a rubber ball out of the box of toys and bounced it, making it hit the microphone on his shorts as interference noise while he spoke. "Sonny and I…" He tossed Dean the ball and he made sure it hit his microphone as well. "…met in the laundry room."

"Dude!" Dean's eyes lit up.

"There's a spot against the wall." Conrad scraped the ball hard on his mike and then bounced it to Dean who did the same. "Under the camera."

"They can see you come and go."

"I know."

"You're out, man." Dean bounced the ball hard, making it leap over their heads.

Conrad caught it, pouting.

"Come inside." Dean took the ball from Conrad, returned it to the box, gesturing for them to enter the house. As they headed to the kitchen, Dean said, "We had a long talk last night, Alfonso and I. We're sick of the game and decided, hell, who cares? I'm not depriving myself of being in his bed every night."

"Holy crap." Conrad stopped him before they joined the others. "Seriously?"

"Yes. I'm sleeping with him from now on. Look. I'm twenty-seven. If my boss at Ink Stains or my family don't like it, tough shit."

Conrad had a new found respect for Dean. "Alfonso feels that way too?"

"Yeah. He figures a gay fitness trainer in the OC isn't exactly as rare as a three dollar bill. Ya know what I mean?"

"Don't you live in Phoenix?"

"For now." Dean's eyes gleamed.

"Guys?" Alfonso called. "Breakfast is on the table."

Conrad instantly realized he was the center of attention when he entered the room. Dean took his usual place next to Alfonso quietly. Before Conrad sat down, he half expected Dean to kiss Alfonso thanking him for the meal. Dean didn't.

Sonny moved the chair out beside him for Conrad.

Something had changed. A presence was in the room, other than Will Markham's spying eye. Did Conrad feel relief? Was the connection between Dean and Alfonso like the dewy mist covering one's body after sex, warm and refreshing? To Conrad it was palpable.

"Thank you for cooking, Alfonso." Conrad slid his chair under the table and picked up his fork.

Tony said in an angry tone, "Okay. What the hell's going on? What did I miss?"

Kelvin instantly perked up. "We missed something?"

"Eat your crepes before they get cold." Alfonso didn't make eye contact.

Sonny elbowed Conrad discreetly, making him catch his gaze. Conrad tried to use mental telepathy to tell him he'd talk to him later.

But the silence at the table was so strained and

misunderstood, Alfonso dropped his fork and said, "Guys…Dean and I—"

Dean slapped his hand over Alfonso's mouth in panic.

"What?" Tony threw up his arms in frustration. "Dean and you are? Are morons? Are insomniacs? Are pissing me off?"

Laughing, Dean said, "Yes, no, yes." He gave Alfonso a warning glare and continued eating.

Okay. Out or not out. That is the question. Conrad thought Alfonso was about to explode. *I'm in a perpetual state of confusion lately.* Conrad assumed from Dean's earlier comments that this was a done deal. Obviously not.

He felt Sonny's elbow again. Conrad shook his head and kept eating.

"Hello, my pets!" Charlotte appeared like a shadow spirit at the threshold. Behind her was a scantily clad beauty holding a box.

"Oh no." Sonny put his fork down and dabbed his mouth with a napkin. "What now?"

She rounded the table, touching each man on the head gently. "We had such a good night last night, didn't we?"

"We did?" Tony's top lip curled. "If someone don't tell me what's going on, I'm going to hurt someone."

Conrad ignored Tony and glanced at the pretty boy holding a box. As if Charlotte caught the direction of Conrad's gaze, she said, "Just set it down in the lounge, Thomas."

Charlotte glided over the tile floor to stand behind Conrad. She pressed cheek to cheek and hung her arms around his chest. "So? I hear Trinity wasn't the girl for you?"

"What do you think?" Conrad avoided Tony's stare from across the table and looked directly at Sonny for support.

"What do I think?" Charlotte squeezed Conrad. "She was strikingly beautiful. I can't imagine why a man wouldn't want her."

"Can't you?" Conrad didn't want to harm Trinity so he kept his real thoughts to himself. It was almost as if Charlotte knew Conrad would have trouble disparaging another human being.

"Why no I can't. She was so willing." Charlotte stood straight. Conrad had to turn in his chair to see what she was doing. Charlotte was smiling at Sonny. "And Conrad didn't even kiss her. Why do you think he didn't, Sonny?"

"Why are you asking me that?" Sonny looked uncomfortable.

"Ask me!" Tony said, "I'll tell ya why. Because Conny's a fucking sissy."

"Oh?" Charlotte crept around the table to Tony like a spider. "Should we set you up with our pretty woman?"

The look on Tony's face made Conrad smile. *Keep talking Tiger. It's your turn.*

With his usual bravado, Tony shrugged, "I'd fuck her. I don't care if she has nuts and boobs."

Dean choked with laughter as Kelvin's eyes went wide as golf balls.

"Care to put your money where your mouth is, Tony?" Conrad felt vindicated.

"Set me up," he replied. "I don't give a shit. It'll give me a chance to get away from these mugs. They're drivin' me nuts."

Before Charlotte replied, Tony added, "But I want a meal out. A good prime rib or Kobe steak."

"He's soooo demanding!" Charlotte batted her lashes and pursed her lips to mock him.

"I didn't even get a drive-thru burger." Conrad finished his crepes.

"Oh, baby," Charlotte teased, "You could have driven through Trinity."

"Ms. Deavers!" Conrad heard the laughter around him and

felt his skin break out in sweat.

"I know, snookums. You're already in love."

Kelvin jerked his head in Conrad's direction quickly.

Conrad hated Charlotte saying anything that may hurt Kelvin's feelings.

"Anyway…" she flipped her wrist in a nonchalant gesture. "Thomas, get the second box as well."

The pretty boy nodded and left through the front door.

Alfonso began clearing plates. Immediately Sonny stood to help him.

"What's the next torture test?" Dean asked, bringing the coffee pot to the table for refills.

"Torture?" Charlotte feigned surprise. "Was that what your night consisted of, Dean?" She ran her fingers down his tattooed arm to his wrist. "Torture?" she purred.

Alfonso began throwing silverware into the sink noisily. Conrad expected the sonic boom of Alfonso's rage at any moment. Maybe Alfonso thought they were comfortable out, but Conrad wasn't so sure Dean shared his opinion.

Pretty Thomas returned hefting another cardboard box. "Where do you want it, Ms. Deavers?"

"It's their chow for the day. Place it on the counter, cutie pie."

Conrad rose up, taking Kelvin's and his plate to the sink. After handing Alfonso the dishes to stow into the washer, Conrad opened the box flaps.

"I hope there's chips in there." Kelvin sat up.

Conrad removed a bag and tossed them to him.

"Yes!" Kelvin pumped his fist.

"You're easy to please." Charlotte took a survey of the men quickly before she asked, "Why hasn't anyone pleased Kelvin? He's as cute as a bottom. Oops! I mean button."

"Huh?" Kelvin blinked and turned a deep shade of

crimson.

"Don't you have somewhere to go?" Conrad nudged Charlotte. "Like the television studio?"

"Are you asking me to leave?" She feigned insult.

"Lord knows," Sonny said, "If we say the wrong thing to Charlotte the consequences will be brutal."

Charlotte spun away from Conrad and pressed her length against Sonny, gazing up at his brown eyes. "As brutal as a mid-night bout of laundry?"

"Will someone tell me what the fuck's goin' on?" Tony rose up and shoved his chair under the table loudly.

"Charlotte, please." Conrad glanced at the three cameras. The kitchen was so loaded with recording devices it was impossible to hide anything.

"The Tiger is in the dark." Charlotte caressed Sonny's shaven head, tugging on his earring. "Did you show Conrad your Z?"

"If that's a euphemism for what I think it is. No."

The fact that Charlotte knew Sonny had a Z tattooed on his dick was almost too much for Conrad to believe. Perhaps during the interview the topic of tattoos had come up. Conrad didn't remember it on a questionnaire.

"His Z?" Tony sincerely looked befuddled. "You have a Z? What, a 240?"

"Is that a car?" Kelvin's naiveté materialized again.

"Agh!" Sonny threw up his hands in fury and stormed out.

The look of contentment on Charlotte's expression was sickening. Conrad crossed the tiled floor and hooked Charlotte's elbow.

"Oh? Are we going for a chat?"

"Yes." Conrad spotted Sonny by the pool so he steered Charlotte into the gym. "Don't hurt Sonny."

"Hurt Sonny?" Charlotte's eyes widened innocently. "Why

would I hurt the man you love?"

Feeling helpless Conrad glanced at the two cameras, one on either side of the room. "Why? Why did you think this premise was a good idea?"

"You can leave anytime, babe. There are no evictions, but none of you are prisoners."

The dare was back. Conrad was not one who liked others to control him. It filled him with resentment. "Who thought of this? You or Will?"

"It's a group effort. Don't you love it?"

Again the cameras caught his eye, then his attention was drawn to Sonny spotting him through the back window, looking frantic.

Because Conrad's gaze darted to the pool area, Charlotte spun around. "There he is. My, isn't he gorgeous? You know, I think he should model. What do you think?"

"Charlotte." Conrad massaged his eyes in agony. "Please. You don't know what you're asking of us."

"Don't I?"

The look of condemnation from her was a surprise. It left Conrad without an answer.

"What am I asking from you, Conrad?" She was dead serious, not joking for once.

"Too much."

"Do you know the struggle that's going on out there? Do I have to list the failed propositions state by state?"

Conrad put his hand over Charlotte's mouth. If she discussed 'Proposition 8' there would no longer be a closet.

Her eyes sparkled. Slowly she dragged his hand away from her face. "I only ask men to be themselves."

"Yes. On *Forever Young*. We know very well what happened to Keith and Carl. It was in every newspaper and tabloid press in the universe." Conrad was cognizant this conversation was not helping hide his sexuality. Sonny's looming concern outside of the glass window was also making him nervous. Making them both nervous.

"Forever Young." She tapped her lip as if the mentioning of her show was perfect. "Yes, let's discuss Keith and Carl, shall we?"

"No." Conrad retreated.

Charlotte latched onto his wrist. "Not so fast. You brought me here to speak in private, you mentioned *Forever Young*. Sit."

Please don't out me, please don't out me. Conrad sat with her on the weight bench.

"Carl Bronson and Keith O'Leary were put through hell because of the tabloid press. The paparazzi were merciless. But…did you watch the Emmys?"

"Of course." Conrad noticed Sonny waving at him frantically, making signs to shut up, including running his finger over his throat as if Conrad was giving them both up. Conrad mouthed, 'Don't worry'.

Charlotte again twirled around to look. "Oh, for cryin' out loud." She stormed outside. Conrad watched her drag Sonny in as if he were headed to a firing squad.

"Oh, God…what's going on?" Sonny cringed.

"Look at the two of you!" Charlotte sat Sonny beside Conrad and shook her head sadly. "I'm ashamed of you both."

"Why?" Sonny squeaked as if his vocal chords were tightening. "What did he tell you?"

"Nothing." Conrad touched Sonny's leg.

Charlotte's attention was drawn to the contact. She crouched down as if to speak confidently which was absurd with so many microphones at hand. "I want you both to observe Dean and Alfonso today."

"Why?" Sonny dabbed at a drop of sweat running down

his temple.

If Conrad thought *he* was afraid of coming out, he couldn't believe how petrified Sonny was. The poor man was running with perspiration.

"Just be observant. Can you do that, med student and construction man?"

Sonny again made anxious eye contact with Conrad. Conrad could read his expression as if he were talking. Sonny obviously had no clue what Conrad had revealed and was going insane.

Charlotte stood, kissed them both on the forehead and said, "There are a lot of men in this world who need positive role models."

"Albert Einstein, Martin Luther King, Abe Lincoln," Sonny rattled off.

"Funny, babe. No. I'm not talking about those kinds. I'm talking about the Keith O'Leary, Carl Bronson, and Mark Antonious Richfield kind."

"Why is she mentioning three gay men?" Sonny whispered into Conrad's ear but Conrad knew Charlotte heard it.

Drawing near, Charlotte caressed Sonny's square jaw affectionately. "What a scholar you are, Sonny. A man who is self-sacrificing, volunteers to fight fires, is an EMT/First Responder, and now wants to be a doctor…they don't get more philanthropic than you. You are everyone's hero. You, Sonny, are the ideal role model."

"No. I'm not. I'm just a moron who got talked into a reality show he didn't know would ruin his life."

With a gallant gesture, Charlotte swept her arm towards the hall. "The exit never locks. If you feel this show has or will ruin you, you are free to go." She paused, arms crossed.

Conrad held his breath thinking Sonny would bolt for the door.

What felt like a long moment passed.

"Ahh, I love it." She smiled in an endearing way. "You'll both be very happy later tonight. Mr. T is going out with his date, and you and the other boys will have your treat all to yourselves."

"What treat?" Sonny asked Conrad.

"She didn't say."

"Bye!" Charlotte vanished, leaving on a trace of her perfume wafting behind her.

Conrad collapsed over his knees and rubbed his face.

"If I don't find out what you two discussed, I'll lose it."

Standing, Conrad signaled for Sonny to follow him upstairs. They heard Charlotte laughing with the other men in the kitchen, a loud reply from Tony of, "I can't wait to get laid," followed.

"Thank fuck he'll be gone for a few hours," Conrad said as he opened the door to his bedroom. Knowing there'd be repercussions for his going against the 'rules', Conrad unhooked his mike and waved Sonny into the bathroom. After Sonny tossed his microphone on the bed with Conrad's, they stood in the tub behind the frosted curtain to whisper in what they knew wasn't privacy but it was the closest thing to it.

"I expect Will's voice to scream any minute." Conrad gave the camera over the door a nervous glance.

"Shut up and tell me what happened."

"She tried the same shit you heard her tell you. I told her nothing about the two of us. She brought up Proposition 8 right before you were dragged in. She's acting like this act of coming out was some big boost to the gay rights ballots."

"You have to be kidding."

"No. I'm not." Conrad lowered his voice even more. "She got downright angry, telling me to watch Alfonso and Dean. I know they've thrown in the towel. They want to have sex while they're here. So? They've pretty much succumbed."

"They did?"

"Dean and Alfonso slept together last night, and Dean said he intends to sleep with him from now on."

Sonny rubbed his hand over his head. "They must have it easier than us."

"Maybe." Conrad stared at Sonny, recalling their oral sex late at night. "How bad would it be for you?"

"Bad." Sonny laughed uneasily. "You?"

"The same. I mean, I get what Charlotte is saying, but I didn't sign up to be her sacrificial lamb."

"Neither did I."

They locked eyes.

Conrad didn't know which of them reacted first, but they lunged for each other. With his powerful build, Sonny forced Conrad to the bottom of the tub in hopes of shielding them from any view of the prying camera.

In the hard ceramic bathtub, Conrad lay on his back with Sonny's weight on top of him. They kissed just like they had the night before; sucking, unbridled twirling tongues and gasping breaths. Conrad's shorts were dragged down his thighs as he tried to do the same to Sonny's. Once their cocks sprang free they ground them together.

"Fuck. Fuck…" Conrad tried to pant quietly but to him it sounded like everything echoed in the tiled stall.

"I want your ass."

Conrad gulped. He'd only been a top. "Shit. I want yours."

Sonny muffled his roar of hilarity.

"Get over here. Jack me off." Conrad held Sonny's jaw and brought him back to his lips.

"I'll do us both." Sonny leaned on one arm and clasped their two erections together. Conrad tried to prop up his head in the tight space; below the spigot and on top of the drain. "Look at that…Look at that!" Conrad admired their dicks nestled side by side.

There was little Conrad could do to help in the cramped spot. Instead, he allowed Sonny to do the work.

Sonny's chest and biceps swelled and rolled as he jacked them off. Conrad was mesmerized by his body and scent. "Baby…close. Close."

"Yeah. Yeah." Sonny increased his hand speed. Soon long, creamy ropes of cum sprayed out of both their slits.

Conrad's body tensed against the ceramic tub and he shut his eyes as it overwhelmed him. A noise scared him out of his wits.

Naked Kelvin climbed on Sonny's back and jacked off against him.

"No! Oh my God!" Sonny looked as if he were having a coronary.

"Kelvin!" Conrad tried to scream quietly.

Cum sprayed all over both Sonny and Conrad as they lay trapped in the bathtub.

"Get the fuck out!" Sonny showed his teeth.

Conrad grabbed Sonny's arm. "Calm down."

After Kelvin slowed his gasping breath, he whispered, "Charlotte told me you'd be doing something and you wanted me to join in."

As slowly and obviously, with as much self-control as he could, Sonny said, "Get. Out."

The look on Kelvin's face was painful for Conrad to see. "It's okay, Kelvin. Just leave, okay?" Conrad felt terrible for him.

"It's not okay." Sonny was livid.

Slinking out, crouching down as he went in an effort to avoid the camera, Kelvin vanished.

Conrad could feel Sonny's rage like boiling heat coming through his skin. "Don't blame the kid. Charlotte put him up to it."

"How'd she know?" Sonny flipped his cock back into his shorts. "Did you tell her we'd done something?"

"No. I told you I didn't tell her shit." Conrad tried to wipe at the spunk he was coated with. "She said something about the laundry room. They saw everything, except the actual act."

"Didn't you tell her we had a talk?" Sonny crouched to allow Conrad to be free so he could stand.

Conrad used a washcloth to clean up. "I tried. She's hell bent on all of us coming out and somehow being the heroes of the reality nation."

Sonny threw back the curtain and stormed out.

"Hey!" Conrad dropped the washcloth and raced after him.

When he caught up to Sonny downstairs, Kelvin was being consoled by Dean and Alfonso in the lounge.

"What the hell is wrong with you guys?" Alfonso asked, holding Kelvin as he sniffled.

Sonny punched a wall. The noise reverberated throughout the house. Conrad was stunned he didn't put a hole through the plaster.

"She told me to do it!" Kelvin's eyes were red rimmed.

Alfonso said softly, "Just what they want for ratings; sex, fighting, and guilt. Bravo! Will, Derek and Charlotte, you got what you were after." He glared at a camera.

Sonny did not look pacified by Alfonso's comments. The pain he was suffering was making Conrad yearn to hold him, help him.

"Look," Sonny held up his finger in warning. "I'm going to the gym because if I don't get this out somehow I'll…" he bit his lip. "No one come in there. Ya got it?"

Conrad nodded. Alfonso, Dean and Kelvin did nothing as Sonny stormed out of the room.

Suddenly Conrad realized someone was missing. "Where's

Tony?"

"Charlotte took him on a shopping spree for an outfit for his date." Dean seemed as if he just noticed the box sitting on the floor that Thomas had left earlier. He knelt down and opened it.

Kelvin said something to Alfonso Conrad couldn't hear, but he thought it was, "I'm okay", or something similar.

Though he wanted to be with Sonny, Conrad respected his need for downtime. He flopped on the couch and felt drained, as if he needed a nap.

"Unreal."

Everyone perked up and looked at Dean.

"What?" Alfonso moved closer to him.

Conrad reached out to Kelvin, indicating for Kelvin to sit with him.

The minute Kelvin did, he cuddled against Conrad's chest. Conrad put his arm around him and held him close.

"A portable DVD player," Dean said as he held it up, setting it on the floor beside him. "And porn."

Alfonso took a DVD package from him. "Gay porn."

Conrad rubbed his forehead. "I can't keep fighting this."

"Don't." Dean passed the film selection for Alfonso to examine. "Like Charlotte said, Conrad, tell the world what a straight macho man you are and leave the house."

Feeling Kelvin shift, Conrad caught him staring at him. "I'm not going anywhere, Kelvin."

Kelvin rested his head against him again, exhaling a loud sigh. "Do you love Sonny?"

"I love all of you guys." Conrad did.

Alfonso smiled and threw Conrad a kiss.

"Is the atmosphere better in here without the Bronx-mouth or what?" Conrad laughed.

A chuckle of approval echoed in the room.

"Let me see those." Conrad stretched to Alfonso who handed him the pile of DVDs he was sifting through.

Sitting up, leaning on Conrad's shoulder, Kelvin inspected the covers and titles as well. "Wow."

"Ever watched porn before?"

"No." Kelvin took one from the pile on Conrad's lap. "Look at the size of him."

Conrad laughed softly.

"I wouldn't want that up my virgin ass."

All three men in the room spun around to Kelvin.

Conrad choked and asked, "Did you come out?"

"Yeah. Fuck it." Kelvin shrugged.

"You're a virgin?" Dean licked his chops.

Alfonso whacked Dean's shoulder. "Down boy."

Suddenly Kelvin went mute and turned red.

"Three down, three to go." Alfonso tossed the few videos he had in his hand back into the box.

At that moment, Sonny appeared, dripping in sweat and his chest so swollen from his workout he made Conrad instantly rock hard.

"Guys."

Conrad sat up.

"I'm going to leave."

"No!" Conrad jumped to his feet.

"Sorry."

When Sonny turned to walk down the hall, Conrad died.

"Go." Dean nudged Conrad to follow.

Sonny wasn't sure of what effect his few days on *Got Men?* had on his real life. But while he was in the gym, working out his anger, he prayed it wasn't already a disaster.

As Sonny walked up the slats to the second floor he could hear footsteps rushing after, and didn't have to turn around to see who it was. He knew.

He walked to the opposite end of the hall as Conrad's room and entered his bedroom. Conrad stood at the doorway, not coming in but obviously wanting to be invited.

"I have to shower." Sonny dropped his gym shorts revealing his briefs.

"Babe." Conrad's voice sounded strangled.

"You can wait out here. I'll be a minute." Sonny took fresh clothing with him to the bathroom and looked back to see Conrad collapsed on his bed, head in hands.

Trying to retain his modesty in a room which should be a private domain even on a reality show, Sonny showered and dressed quickly. When he returned to his bedroom, Conrad was in the same position he had left him, hunched over on his bed.

Sonny removed his suitcase from the closet and began packing until he heard a sob. Jerking around to Conrad, Sonny felt a stabbing pain in his chest. "Don't make this any harder than it is."

"Sorry…" Conrad choked, hiding in his hands, trying to look invisible, though his six foot height and two-hundred-plus pounds made it impossible.

"I have to. You know I do." Sonny tried not to get emotional. If he thought about Conrad's pain he'd fall apart.

"One more day?" Conrad cried, rubbing at his eyes as if the tears infuriated him.

"I'm already dead. This show has probably killed me. I have to find out what's going on in the outside world. I can't feel sick for another two weeks wondering what my family thinks, what my co-workers think…how my studies will be affected."

Conrad nodded, but didn't look at him.

Sonny didn't even know Conrad's last name, and didn't have a pen or paper to write any of his home info down. Besides, he lived in Philly and Conrad lived in Elk Grove. What was the point?

Before Sonny said another word, Conrad staggered to his feet, reaching like a blind man to the door. He left Sonny's room and Sonny could hear his soft tread down the hall, then a door close at the end.

Continuing to pack, Sonny felt his heart break. But he had no choice.

Chapter Nine

Lying on his face, his arms tucked under his pillow, Conrad's tears had dried and his mind was blank. He heard the footsteps past his door, the voices below, then the front door of the house close.

A light tap sounded at his door but Conrad didn't have the strength to answer. He listened to it open and three men sat on the bed next to him, caressing his back and stroking his hair gently. With an effort, Conrad moved to lie on his side to see his loyal housemates.

Alfonso's dark, patient gaze was the first Conrad met.

Instantly Alfonso embraced Conrad, holding him tight. While Conrad held him for dear life, he heard Kelvin's sniffle and Dean's loud distressed sigh.

"Babe." Alfonso kissed Conrad's neck a few times. "It's okay."

Mouthing 'no' Conrad's voice had failed him. His throat was so constricted he couldn't speak.

"Come down and eat." Dean combed his fingers through Conrad's hair.

"Not hungry." Conrad had to force words of communication.

"Please." Kelvin held Conrad's hand, looking sick with worry.

"There's booze." Alfonso wiped Conrad's dewy forehead and palmed his jaw, meeting his eyes. "Come down with us."

"Is the asshole back?"

"No. Hopefully they'll keep him out all night." Alfonso began coaxing Conrad to stand.

Aching, stiff and weary, Conrad allowed the three to help him rise. With their hands touching, squeezing and escorting him, Conrad made his way to the kitchen and sat on a stool at the counter. Alfonso placed a bottle of vodka and a shot glass in front of him. Dean poured a round for all of them.

"What time is it?" Conrad felt disoriented.

"Nearly five." Dean moved the shot closer to Conrad, encouraging him to drink it.

"What? How can that be?"

"You must have fallen asleep," Dean said.

"He did." Kevin raised his glass. "I checked on him."

Conrad downed the vodka and choked at the potency.

"I'm making pizza. What do you like on it?" Alfonso began removing ingredients from the fridge and cabinets.

"I'm not hungry."

Dean refilled the empty glasses. "Anything is good, Alfonso."

"Pizza," Kelvin said softly, caressing Conrad's cheek. "Nothing's as good as pizza."

"Homemade pizza." Alfonso smiled.

Dean pressed his lips to Conrad's ear. "Pizza and porno, yum."

Conrad laughed though it felt strained. "Thanks, guys. You're awesome."

"You won't leave now, will you, Conrad?" Kelvin's eyes watered.

"No." Conrad rubbed Kelvin's back. "I'm not going. I'm

sticking it out with you guys."

A big smile on his face, Kelvin wrapped his arm around Conrad and rested his head on his shoulder. "You're the best."

"Goat cheese, spinach, walnuts, roasted garlic, sun-dried tomatoes and grated asiago." Alfonso spun the dough with the backs of his knuckles.

"What?" Kelvin sat up. "Pizza, Alfonso. You know, pepperoni, sausage, tomato sauce, gooey cheese…"

Dean met Conrad's eye and they both laughed in amusement.

"Ah, young stud, you have so much to learn," Alfonso replied, giving Kelvin a wink.

Sated on gourmet pizza, vodka and beer, with Kelvin attached to his side, Conrad slouched on the sofa, staring at the miniature DVD screen but not really seeing it. They had it facing away from any camera so the content of the films could not be seen, and it was on mute. They didn't have to hear it. Other than campy music and grunts, there was no dialogue. Conrad didn't get horny watching porn stars hump, he got lonely.

By eleven the sound of the door moving caught everyone's attention. Dean paused the video and Conrad hopped to his feet, "Sonny?"

Tony appeared, grinning like the devil incarnate, his face ruddy and his clothing disheveled.

The second Conrad realized who it was, he returned to his spot on the sofa.

"Boys! Boys! Boys!" Tony opened his arms like he was hamming it up on a stage. "What a night!"

"Yeah?" Dean asked.

"Tits and cock!" Tony made a face of ecstasy.

"You do realize you just told the world what you did."

Alfonso laughed.

"Hey." Tony threw up his hands. "If it has a hole, I'll fuck it. I'm a free man. I'm divorced, no kids…"

"You're a teacher!" Conrad shook his head.

"Maybe after this, I'll be a star." Tony removed his suit jacket and shoes. "You know, like them pop stars on those crappy singing shows. Those guys get all sorts of offers."

Kelvin's jaw was hanging open. "Did you say you really did it with someone like that?"

"Mm!" Tony grabbed his crotch and pumped it. "Fucked and fucked…"

"Okay. I'm going to be ill." Kelvin's nose crinkled.

"Hey." Tony looked around. "Where's sunshine? In the toilet?"

"He left." Dean glanced at Conrad.

"Left?" Tony unbuttoned his cuffs. "What did you do, Conny? You asshole."

Conrad tensed and Kelvin grabbed his arm to keep him on the sofa.

"Sonny had things to do in the outside world so he had to leave." Alfonso waved his hand. "So? You and this woman going to hook up again?"

"Frig no." Tony laughed as if the idea were absurd. "Let me strip outta' this monkey suit. Then I want to hear what Conny did to chase Sonny out."

Once Tony left the room, Conrad breathed fire.

"Ignore him," Dean said, "You do realize he wants a rise out of you."

"I need to kill someone anyway." Conrad clenched his fists.

"No." Kelvin attached himself to Conrad's arm. "No fighting."

"You want him humping your leg like a dog?" Alfonso

asked. After leaning over in his chair, peeking down the hall, Alfonso added, "I bet Tony didn't even touch that woman."

Conrad shook his head. "No way. He screwed her."

"Uh uh. My guess?" Alfonso glanced down the hall once more. "He couldn't get it up with someone like that. He likes macho men. Macho men who rough him up."

Dean choked in a laugh.

Conrad thought about it. "You think this screwing talk is bravado?"

"Fuck yeah." Alfonso nodded as if reinforcing his view. "Look at him. No way. He wrestles with you, the biggest most masculine guy in here," Alfonso pointed to Conrad, "and you think he's going to make it with a tranny with tits? Ha!"

Dean gestured with his hands at the futility. "No way to know. Tony's never going to admit it."

"Bet he tells his personal diary cam."

"No!" Conrad gasped. "Alfonso, you can't look at that."

"Why not?" Alfonso shrugged. "The world is."

Kelvin whispered, "Yeah, but even on that thing, Tony would lie."

Standing, Alfonso peeked around the corner of the wall. "I know how we can verify it."

"How?" Dean asked.

When Alfonso met Conrad's eye, Conrad shook his head. "Oh, no. No way."

"We'll leave you alone with him. Pick a fight. When you're on the floor and he's grinding, ask him. Tell him you won't fuck him if he fucked a he/she."

"He'll lie." Conrad shivered. "He'll lie to get what he wants."

"No. I swear, if you ask him at the right moment, he just might come clean." Alfonso dove onto his chair.

Everyone shut up.

Tony, wearing just a pair of shorts, rubbed his hands together. "So? You all missed a T-bone steak. What did you eat? Granola? Salad?"

"Homemade pizza." Kelvin sat up. "It even had some stuff on it I never heard of. But it was awesome."

Tony seemed to sense something. He stared at each of them, one by one.

"I'm tired." Alfonso stood, stretched, played up a yawn and looked back at Dean.

"Me too." Dean shut off the DVD player and leapt to his feet. "Gee, Kelvin, aren't you tired?"

"Huh?" Kelvin tilted his head. "Oh!" He pecked Conrad on the cheek. "Night."

Conrad panicked, wanting to call them back as they gave him wicked glances and left.

"So?" Tony crossed his arms. "What the fuck did ya do to our token black guy? Ya fucking dick."

In the mood Conrad was in, it didn't take much provoking. He rose to his feet and pointed a warning finger in Tony's direction. "Don't start."

"Me?" Tony made a face of innocence. "I've been gone all day, your buddy Sonny's not here, and when I ask what the fuck you did, you boner, you get smart with me?"

"Leave me alone." The minute Conrad tried to walk passed Tony, Tony shoved him. It was becoming a repetitive script. Now it was up to Conrad whether to take the bait. If he was honest with himself, he needed to pummel someone.

"I'm warning you." Conrad gave Tony one more out before things grew violent.

"Warning me?" Tony puffed up and threw up his hands in a classic gesture of battle ready he'd used before. "You pussy. You can't even fuck someone who's given it to you on a silver platter. You need blue pills or something, macho man?"

“That’s it.” Conrad didn’t need any more of an excuse. He pounced. Tony didn’t expect the attack and slammed against a wall. As Conrad drew back for a punch aimed at Tony’s jaw, Tony gripped Conrad’s wrist to stop it.

They growled like fighting pitbulls, both foaming at the mouth to kill. Conrad managed to get his hands around Tony’s throat and they tumbled over the coffee table and onto the floor. With a grip on both of Conrad’s wrists, Tony wrenched the hold back enough to not choke. “You want me. That’s why you sent Sonny packing. To get him out of our way.”

“God! I hate you!” Conrad knew Tony couldn’t be more wrong.

“You don’t hate me, you pussy.” Tony ground his crotch against Conrad and Conrad could feel Tony’s cock was so hard it was like iron.

Resisting the urge to twist away and not feel that erection he loathed, Conrad had a strange feeling the others had drawn near yet out of sight. He knew Alfonso and Dean would never let them really hurt each other. At least that’s what Conrad assumed. So, he played the game.

“I wouldn’t fuck you,” Conrad sneered, but he ground his groin into Tony’s to urge him on. Conrad, however, was not hard.

“Yeah, you would.” Tony spread his legs and dry humped Conrad so roughly it was painful.

“Not after your dick was in that he/she.” Conrad stared directly into Tony’s dark eyes.

“I used a rubber.” Tony shifted his hips and jammed his stiff dick against Conrad’s groin.

“I don’t give a shit if you used a body bag. You’re not coming near me after that.” Conrad growled and pushed Tony away.

“I didn’t fuck her!” Tony said, “I don’t want anything to do with tits or make up or nuthin female!”

"Why did you tell us you did?" Conrad suddenly felt sorry for this man. The image, the denial. How difficult was this on Tony? Conrad was beginning to see this charade was just as miserable for Tony thc Tiger as it was for Sonny and him.

"I said it for the boys, for the fucking camera," Tony whispered in Conrad's ear, licking it.

"Stop." Conrad couldn't take the contact anymore. "Stop!" He threw Tony off of him and tried to get to his feet.

The housemates surrounded them to break it up.

"Oh, I fucked and fucked," Dean mocked, rubbing his crotch.

"Lay off him." Conrad was growing very unhappy with the group. What had been supportive was beginning to deteriorate. Conrad didn't say goodnight as he went to his room. All he wanted was Sonny. What was the point of being here without him?

Alone in his room Conrad picked up the diary cam and pointed it at his face. "I want out."

Chapter Ten

Yes the clock read ten, but Conrad could not motivate to get out of bed. It had been twenty-four hours since his baby had left.

Kelvin had knocked an hour ago, asking if he was coming down for breakfast. Conrad said, "No, thank you."

Envisioning himself packing, going home, Conrad was amazed he'd be giving up after less than a week. But no one warned him what the show was about. No one told him the man he wanted to get to know on a very deep level would bail, leaving him to carry on with four housemates. Two, a loving couple; one, an innocent virgin who idolized him; and the last, an antagonistic suitor. *Lucky me*.

Another knock at his door annoyed him. "Go away."

"You sure?"

Conrad bolted upright. "No!"

"Yeah."

When Conrad heard Sonny's laugh, he flew off the bed and opened the door. He didn't care who saw. Conrad hugged him, picking him up off his feet. He buried his nose into Sonny's neck and inhaled, rocking him in his arms.

"I missed you too." Sonny rubbed their rough cheeks together. "Now put me down!" Sonny laughed and whacked Conrad's shoulder.

As if suddenly realizing he was still on camera, Conrad dropped Sonny back to the floor and mouthed, 'I am so sorry!'

"No. I owe you the apology. Come here." Sonny marched through Conrad's bedroom to the bathroom.

Conrad hadn't put his microphone on yet, so he stood in the tub with Sonny, closed the curtain and they crouched down to whisper.

"My family figured it out." Sonny caressed Conrad's cheek. "They said with what they were showing on television, which believe me, even on primetime is incriminating, they knew."

Conrad died.

"Listen to me." Sonny ran his hand behind Conrad's neck to the nape. "I thought, Oh my God, I'll be crucified, you know?"

His eyes burning, Conrad paid close attention.

"To my absolute astonishment, my family said they suspected I was gay. Even my dad." Sonny glanced through the frosted curtain to where they both knew a camera was. He lowered his voice, barely audible. "When I showed up in Philly, they were stunned. They grew angry at me for abandoning you guys. They turned me around within five minutes and put me back on a plane."

"No!" Conrad dabbed at his eyes.

"I swear." Sonny held up his hand in an oath. "I called the boys at the fire station. They gave me some shit, but didn't care. Even my captain told me he was pissed off I left the show. That I abandoned *you*."

Conrad mouthed, 'Oh my God.'

"I'm out." Sonny shrugged. "But I know you're not. The housemates told me you've been sulking since I left."

"I was." Conrad toyed with Sonny's fingers. "I was imagining packing. I didn't want to stay if you weren't here."

"Yeah, but…will you still be afraid?"

"I am. I'm petrified."

"What if your family is reacting the same way as mine, and you just don't know it?"

"Hello, boys."

In terror, Conrad felt his heart explode in his chest as Charlotte pushed back the shower curtain.

"No microphones? Hiding in the tub? Naughty, naughty!" She wagged her finger. "At least celebrate with a good romp in bed."

"Charlotte. What are we going to do with you?" Sonny stepped out of the bathtub.

"Obey my rules!" she announced in a playful tone. Her gaze turned to Conrad. "I assume this means you're staying."

"What are you clairvoyant?" Conrad climbed out of the bathtub.

"Yes. I know and see all…" She moved her hands as if she had an imaginary crystal ball. "Go. Microphones. Now."

Sonny gave Conrad a sexy smile over his shoulder.

It melted Conrad completely.

Charlotte just about jumped in glee when she spied it. "I love my boys!" she cheered as she skipped out of the room.

With his hands on Sonny's shoulders from behind, Conrad followed him down the stairs to the others.

Alfonso and Dean appeared very pleased with Sonny's return. Conrad noticed a slight downturn in Kelvin's smile while Tony didn't hide his jealousy.

"What's the daily torture?" Alfonso asked before Charlotte raced out.

"Just behave. Stop taking your microphones off and hiding in the bathtub." Charlotte slanted her eyes at Conrad and Sonny. "Rules are rules."

"Bathtub?" Tony asked. "Why do I feel like I'm always missin' shit?"

Charlotte sauntered across the tiled floor to Tony, draping her arm around his neck. "Sugarplum? Don't talk about 'missin' shit', okay? We all know the opportunity you passed up."

Tony's cheeks went crimson.

Sonny tilted his head to Conrad curiously. Conrad mouthed, 'Tell ya later'.

"If you're all good. Or bad," she said as she made the rounds of eye contact, "I have a very big surprise for all of you."

"A hamburger and fries?" Kelvin asked sarcastically.

"Is that what you really want, baby?" Charlotte made her way to Kelvin, who flinched at her approach as if he were petrified of her.

"I wouldn't mind."

"How about this instead?" She pressed her mouth to Kelvin's ear and whispered.

Conrad watched Kelvin's face light up.

"No!" Kelvin gasped.

"But if you tell," Charlotte turned her back on him. "I call it off."

"You're cruel!" Kelvin laughed, but Conrad could see he was serious.

"Bye!" Charlotte left.

All eyes rested on Kelvin.

"Oh no. I can't. Guys. If I tell you and she cancels it, I'm going to slit my wrists."

Alfonso swooped towards Kelvin. "Tell!"

"No!" Kelvin smiled, backing up.

"Now!" Dean edged closer.

With a roar of laughter, Kelvin raced out of the house

through the sliding door.

A minute later Conrad heard three loud cannonball splashes into the pool.

About to say something to Sonny, Conrad realized Tony was standing there, watching them. "Uh." Conrad gestured to the back of the house. "Go?"

"Are you guys together or what?' Tony was neither smiling nor sneering. It seemed as if he were after a fact.

Sonny met Conrad's gaze.

Ice filled Conrad's blood but he didn't deny it.

"Pussies." Tony left the room.

"He's got it bad for you."

"I don't know what he's got," Conrad said, "But I don't want it."

Sonny laughed, then reached out to lead Conrad to the sectional in the lounge. They relaxed together, each with one leg bent under them, facing one another. Conrad leaned his elbow on the back of the sofa to prop up his chin in his palm. "Tony went out with that post-op tranny last night."

Sonny grinned mischievously.

"He came back all cocky, telling us how he fucked her."

"Yeah, huh." Sonny's eyebrow raised.

"Alfonso asked me to get to the truth. They left me alone with him, which never ends well."

"You two have another sparring match?"

"We did. After you left, I was ready to kill someone. And he volunteered."

The smile dropped from Sonny's lips. "I'm sorry."

"Don't be. Anyway, Tony took the bait of course. He was humping me so hard I swear my crotch is sore this morning."

Using his hand to cover his smile, Sonny choked, holding back his laugh.

"I told him I wouldn't go near him if he touched that woman. So, he said he didn't."

"He's all fucking talk."

"Sonny." Conrad touched Sonny's leg. "He's just as terrified as we are. Look, the guy's a divorced teacher putting on the Bronx macho act. This has got to be the hardest on him. None of us knew what we were signing on to here."

A look of surprise washed over Sonny's face. "Yeah. That's true. He's doing his damnedest to keep the myth alive."

"They can't fire him for being gay. That's not politically correct."

"But could you imagine? What if his family is like the Sopranos?" Sonny exaggerated a shiver.

"We need to keep cool about it. Poor guy. He'll end up in a lead suit buried in Giants' stadium."

Sonny cracked up with laughter.

When Conrad spied it, he fell more in love. With his hand covering his mouth to shield the camera from reading his lips, Conrad mumbled, "Two tops?"

"I will break you." Sonny's sexuality was sizzling.

"Will you?"

"Yes. You will be my bottom boy."

Conrad cracked up with laughter and slumped down low on the sofa. "I want to fuck you. Now," he breathed as softly as he could.

"Come out. Let's hit the bed."

Kelvin's shriek of pleasure echoed through the house, followed by more splashing.

"What are those boys up to?"

Conrad didn't care. He was considering Sonny's offer.

As if Sonny could read his mind, he asked, "What's your biggest fear?"

"My brothers and my dad. I'm beginning to care less and less about my bar buddies."

"Are they religious?"

"Not overly. We're sort of Catholic but we don't go to church."

"What's your last name?" Sonny whispered close to Conrad's ear.

"Hogan. Yours?"

"Washington." Sonny licked his top lip. "You get me so hot."

Conrad glanced around the room and up at the cameras again. "You…uh…you ever been with a white guy?"

"Yeah. You ever had a black man as your partner?"

"No. But, man, do I want one now." Conrad blew out a breath and rolled his eyes comically.

Chuckling, Sonny asked, "What are you looking for? Where are you in your life?"

"Shit." Conrad ground his jaw. "I hate this conversation being filmed."

"Bathtub?" Sonny grinned.

"No." Conrad ran his hand through his hair in frustration and decided to just talk. "I want something serious. I had a partner who didn't. He told me," Conrad cleared his throat, "*She* told me she wasn't ready for something monogamous. At least I wasn't lied to. It was all up front. But I was not happy."

"How do you feel about long distance relationships?"

"I'm not keen."

Tony's voice carried into the house, "You will pay for that, babycakes!" followed by everyone's laughter and more water splashing.

Pausing to listen, Conrad refocused on Sonny. "I can move. I have no job, and I know you can't leave med school."

"Are you there?" Sonny sat up, appearing surprised.

"Where?" Conrad tilted his head.

"Moving already?"

Instantly Conrad felt like a fool. His face went burning hot and he avoided Sonny's dark eyes.

"Conrad."

He blinked as Sonny touched his knee.

"I'd love it," Sonny said.

"We still have two weeks here. Two weeks, twenty-four/seven. If that doesn't make or break a relationship, nothing will."

"With you in my bed, or?"

Again Conrad took a paranoid glance at the camera. "I wish I had the opportunity that you did to go out of this house and see for myself the damage."

"Then do it."

Out of thin air, Will's voice replied, "No. I'm sorry. No more exits with returns."

Conrad felt the hair rise on his neck that every word they were saying had indeed been heard.

"Let's go check on the others." Sonny hit Conrad's leg with the back of his hand and stood.

Conrad nodded, following him out, giving the camera a scowl of anger.

The other four were in the pool dunking each other, throwing beach balls and Styrofoam noodles and having a blast.

Conrad sighed deeply, wondering if he was the last holdout of the group who felt the weight of the world on his back. When Sonny stripped down to his gym shorts and joined the fray, Conrad knew he was indeed, the last one.

Chapter Eleven

Now that Sonny had invited Conrad to his bed, it was up to him to make the move.

Lying with his hands behind his head, staring at the ceiling at its light patterns from the pool spot lamps out back, Conrad was torn.

Mom, Dad, I'm gay.

How many times did he yearn to say that? He was twenty-seven, never brought home a woman, didn't go to any of his school proms…were they stupid?

He wrote poetry, loved musical theater, art, mushy romance movies…hello?

The only reason he was into construction was because his dad and brothers were. His father owned his own business and since Conrad was sixteen he worked for him. It was only within the last year that his father's contracts had dried up. The downturn in the economy destroyed his father's business. Bankrupted him.

So now they were all doing odd jobs for other companies. Life was not good at the Hogan household. Conrad had a hunch, if Sonny's family had figured it out, so had his. It made Conrad want to flee to Philly just so he didn't have to face his worst nightmare; his family's condemnation.

Would they be cool?

"No."

He tossed and turned, unable to sleep. Under the sheet he held his cock and couldn't focus enough to jack off. All that ended up doing was making him angry.

Sonny was down at the end of the hall. Waiting. No, they didn't have rubbers or lube, but some kissing and sucking would be fabulous. Holding Sonny all night in his arms after coming would certainly help him sleep.

Alfonso and Dean were most likely spent, out like a light, sated, falling madly in love as their bodies intertwined.

Conrad punched the pillows in anger, tearing at the bedding, unable to get comfortable.

The war in his head was unrelenting.

Charlotte's words, her encouragement to be himself, show the world it was okay and that gay men didn't have to hide echoed in his temples. Keith O'Leary, Carl Bronson, Mark Richfield, all men in the spotlight, all out. O-U-T. How did their families react? How did they cope? How did they do it?

"Their lovers," Conrad whispered. "Their lovers' support got them through."

That had to be the key. That way when the family alienated you like you were a leper, you had someone to cling to to get through it. Someone like Sonny.

Not only did Conrad have to battle the sexual stereotyping, his family had to cross racial lines as well, and that included his homophobic brothers.

How could they judge Sonny? The guy was a med student and a firefighter. Would they? Could they?

Sonny's too good for me. That's the fucking irony. When the guy's got his diploma on the wall and is making a million a year, what will he want with an unemployed construction worker with just a high school degree?

Growling out loud, Conrad could not sleep. He wrestled with the blankets until he was out from under them, stood up, and headed down the stairs. Lingering at the back slider, he gazed at the pool envisioning the six of them playing in it.

Heading to the kitchen, he opened the fridge but wasn't hungry. When the light from inside the refrigerator illuminated the room, he nearly jumped out of his skin to see Tony.

Tony was seated at the dining room table, an empty glass and a bottle of scotch in front of him.

Conrad closed the door and sat beside him. Tony's eyes were watery and glazed. He reached for Tony's hand and held it.

Tears ran from Tony's eyes when he blinked.

"We're the last two holdouts."

"I'm dyin here. I don't know what the fuck to do." Tony wiped his eyes roughly with his free hand.

"Me neither. I feel as if I'm fucked anyway and I may as well just go for it."

"Yeah. Me too." Tony released Conrad's hand and poured more scotch, holding out the bottle in offer.

Conrad nodded, getting himself a glass and returning.

Tony filled it.

"Thanks."

They tapped the glasses and shot down the liquor.

Conrad placed the empty on the table and leaned on his elbows. "How is your family about it? Do you know how they'd react?"

"They'd kill me." Tony laughed but it was tortured not happy. "I used to live in Dayton when I was married. I should have stayed there or moved to California, anywhere but New York."

"How hard would it be to get a teaching job somewhere else? Away from your family?"

"I don't know. I just hate the idea of being on my own. Starting over again." Tony refilled his glass.

Conrad put his hand over his to stop him. "I'm good."

"I fell for a guy in Ohio." Tony's lips tightened to a thin line. "I was still married at the time. We met while we were members in a bike club. A bunch of us went to Sturgis."

"I remember you mentioning it to Dean."

"Loved him. Gorgeous fucker." Tony's hands shook as he picked up the shot glass. "Dev Young. He writes erotic fiction."

"What happened?"

Tony shot down the booze and waited for the fire to pass before he answered. "Fell in love with someone else. Like you did."

Conrad felt guilt in the pit of his stomach. "You don't exactly woo lovers, Tony."

"Not my style." Tony shrugged. "I like a good fight." He smiled but it faded. Tony rubbed his eyes and face, Conrad could see how conflicted he was. "I'm going to get a good fight when I get out of here." Tony exhaled loudly. "I'll be shot execution style."

"Don't say that. You can't be serious."

"Look." Tony met Conrad's eyes. "I had no idea when I got on this show what it was about. Did you?"

"No."

He threw up his hands. "It was done so we'd come out and make fools of ourselves, or join some cause to right the wrongs of society. I know that now. Would I have done this show if I'd have known? Hell no." Tony wiped his mouth with the back of his hand. "My mother sleeps with a rosary, a bible on her nightstand. Okay? My family keeps to their own. I can't even head back there when I leave here. I have to go somewhere else. And if I'm lucky, I won't have a contract on my head."

"You have to be kidding me."

He shrugged. "I'm guessin', like you are. Do you know what you're going back to when this is done?"

Conrad shivered. “No.”

“You an’ me. We’re in the same boat. The rest either don’t live near their relatives, or they don’t have the threat of homicide on their heads. I don’t know. Me? I’m scared shitless.”

“Me too.”

“You an’ Sonny goin’ to be together?”

Conrad took a paranoid look at the camera. “We’ll be good friends, sure.”

“Shit. Sorry.”

When Tony went to pour another shot, Conrad asked, “How many of those did you have?”

“Lost count.”

Moving the bottle, Conrad capped it and put it out of Tony’s reach.

“Why do you care about me? I’ve treated you like shit.”

“Because I finally figured out why. We’re not so different, you and me.”

“No. We’re not. In the same damn boat.” Tony scrubbed his eyes.

“It’s fucking late. Come on. Even if we can’t sleep, we have to rest.” Conrad stood, hauling Tony with him. They walked silently, holding each other.

Once they were upstairs, Tony paused. “Listen.”

Conrad strained to hear. A very soft, “Oh yeah…” came from Alfonso’s room.

“Well, Dean’s getting some, that’s for sure.” Conrad chuckled and led Tony to his door.

“Thanks for bein’ there, Conrad.”

Conrad held Tony’s face and smiled at him. “You got it, Tiger. Anytime you need me, I’m there.” Conrad added, “As a friend.”

Tony gave him a sly smile. “I’ve heard that before. From Dev.”

“See ya.” Conrad stepped backwards, allowing Tony to walk away.

“See ya.” Tony entered his room, closing the door.

Conrad took a long look down the hallway to Sonny’s room, turned and headed to his own bed.

Chapter Twelve

Conrad woke to Kelvin's noisy exclamations. He couldn't understand his words but the tone was obvious.

After only getting a few hours of real sleep, Conrad showered and shaved, wondering what Charlotte had planned that was making Kelvin bounce off the walls.

He met Tony on his way down. It seems he and the Tiger were the only ones late to wake, both having a bad night. They exchanged smiles. Peace at last.

"Amazing what common ground can do, eh, Tony?" Conrad caressed his hair affectionately.

"Yeah. We should keep up the act though. I think it gets the other guys hot."

"Get over here, ya monster." Conrad embraced him, kissing his neck. In Tony's ear he whispered, "You're just a softie. I know your secret now."

"Not where it counts." Tony grabbed Conrad's ass and thrust his hard cock into his crotch.

Conrad gave him a playful scolding glance and began his descent to the main floor. "What the hell has Kelvin so crazy?"

"No clue."

Conrad headed directly to the coffee pot and poured two, handing a mug to Tony. "What's the deal, Kelvin? Finally getting bacon and homefries for breakfast?"

"No! No!" Kelvin bounced like a rabbit, his ponytail flipping around in circles.

"Jesus Christ, babycakes," Tony said, sipping the coffee. "Someone get him a tranquilizer."

Sonny sidled up to Conrad. "You and Tony seem…human?"

"Yeah. Shh." Conrad winked.

The front door opened with a slight clatter. It drew the attention of the housemates. As they hovered in the hall Ms. Deavers led a crew inside.

"My boys!" she gushed. "All awake and ready for action, eh?"

"Yeah, but there's no food." Alfonso rested against Dean's back.

"Oh! Who knew you'd all be so hungry you'd eat us out of house and home." She shuffled a few men with equipment into the hall. "Thomas? Oh, pretty boy, Thomas?" she called outside. "Get the two boxes marked 'chow'. My men are hungry."

"Does your husband know you have an appetite for young boys?" Dean asked, slanting his eyes at her.

"Hey, no crime in looking." She met Kelvin's gaze. "Right my twinkie-poo?"

"Do I even want to ask what that means?" Kelvin cringed.

Both Sonny and Conrad said 'No', in harmony.

"Don't you love virgin territory?" Charlotte rubbed her hands in glee.

Thomas muscled past the group holding a box. He set it on the counter in the kitchen and left for the second one.

Alfonso opened the flaps to have a look.

"When is he coming here?" Kelvin asked Charlotte, appearing exasperated. "I haven't said anything to anyone."

Before Charlotte replied to Kelvin, Kelvin began sniffing

the air like a bloodhound. “That guy! He’s wearing it!”

Tony shook his head. “Please, give the kid a valium.”

Charlotte held Kelvin’s chin in her hand. “So smart! Gold star for you.”

Sonny asked, “What the fuck are they talking about?”

“That’s not all you got, Kelvin.” Alfonso held up a package of turkey bacon.

“Yes! Yes!” Kelvin danced around.

“So easy to please.” Charlotte laughed. “Wish all men were that way.”

When she connected to Conrad’s gaze, he froze. “Don’t start on me.”

“Two left,” she said as she spun towards the door, holding up her fingers.

Conrad and Tony exchanged nervous looks at her head count.

Thomas entered the house with another box and placed it next to the first. Kelvin rushed him, sniffing him like a rabid animal. Thomas shrunk back. “What the hell’s the matter with you?”

“*Dangereux* Cologne. You’re wearing it.” Kelvin moaned.

Sonny and Conrad exchanged puzzled glances.

Suddenly Dean said, “Oh… I get it.”

“Enlighten us, Deano.” Tony refilled his cup from the pot of coffee.

“Mark Antonious Richfield.”

Conrad blew out his coffee again, choking. “No-fucking-way.”

“Way.” Kelvin gloated, crossing his arms over his chest and rocking on his heels. “That’s what I wasn’t allowed to tell you guys.”

“He’s coming here?” Sonny pointed to the camera crew

out at the pool.

"Yup!" Kelvin did another happy dance.

"Is that the guy that did the three-way on *Forever Young*?" Tony asked. "He looks like a girl."

"Uh. No." Dean smiled. "He doesn't look like a girl. He's the hottest fucking model on the planet."

"Uh hum?" Alfonso was standing at the stove, cooking up bacon and eggs. The scent was beginning to fill the room.

"Not as hot as you," Dean said, then made a silly face.

"Shut up and set the table."

Dean laughed as he obeyed.

Sonny glanced at Conrad. "They are treating us well. Keith and Carl, Mark Richfield?"

"Yeah, all Charlotte's gay role models." Conrad made a fresh pot of coffee. "I'm waiting for Will Markham and Madison Henning to come by and screw on the couch."

"Don't tempt me," Will's reply sent a chill up Conrad's spine. Just when he forgot the cameras existed, that omnipresent voice reminded him.

"Anyway…She has a point." Sonny handed Conrad the bag of coffee grounds. "All those men are in the spotlight and openly gay. You have to admit that's not easy."

Conrad glanced above Sonny's head to the camera lens. "Ya think?" he said sarcastically.

"I've read stuff about Mark." Kelvin sat at the stool but it was as if he was going to squirm off he was so excited. "He did a bio in one of the gay men's mags. He said his dad was really a bastard and beat him into acting straight."

"Ouch." Sonny cringed, setting milk out on the counter.

Dean continued to place flatware around the table. "I heard he was about to get married, like standing at the altar with a woman, when his lover swept him off his feet."

"Shut up!" Conrad laughed. All the men stared at him with

serious expressions. “You’re not kidding me?”

“No. I’m not.” Dean put the napkin holder in the middle of the table. “Uh…some ex-LAPD cop.”

“Steve Miller.” Kelvin licked his lips. “Man, that bacon smells good.”

“I bet he don’t look as good in person.” Tony leaned back on the counter. “They airbrush the shit out of those model-types.”

“We’ll soon see.” Sonny loaded the toaster with bread.

Conrad noticed Kelvin off in a dream world. “Bet you have a poster of him on your bedroom wall.”

“Yup.” Kelvin smiled.

“Do you live at home, Kelvin?” Dean asked.

“No. I share a place in Belltown with a female friend. She’s a hairdresser.”

“Belltown?” Tony put his coffee mug in the sink.

“It’s an area of downtown Seattle.”

“Never been to Seattle,” Conrad said. “Does it really rain a lot?”

“Constantly!” Kelvin hopped off the stool. “When do you think he’s coming?”

“Who? Mark?” Sonny buttered the toast as they popped up, filling the slots with more bread.

“Yes, duh.”

Alfonso said, “Sunny-side up, scrambled, poached…come and get it.”

“You poached my eggs?” Tony gasped.

“Yeah. What the hell.” Alfonso held them up in a slotted spoon. “Hop to it!”

Tony grabbed a plate and hustled over.

Sonny put a stack of toast on the table and held out his dish for his breakfast, giving Conrad a wink as he did.

Conrad wondered. If Mark Richfield could come out with an ex-LAPD cop, could he?

The photographer arrived first. A woman, similar to Charlotte in appearance, in her early forties, petite, yet powerful in aura and presence, entered the house. She held out her hand for greetings, "Janis Campbell, nice to meet you."

One by one the men shook her hand. Kelvin had his face plastered to the front window soon after.

"Where?" Janis asked an assistant.

"Out back." A young man raced in front of her, showing her the way.

Conrad stood behind Kelvin, rubbing his back. "You do realize he'll be here all of five minutes."

"I don't care. He's my idol."

"Is that why you have a ponytail?" Conrad tugged on it playfully.

"Yes. Stop." Kelvin swatted his hand away.

Sonny touched Conrad's arm, tilting his head for him to follow. When they were 'alone' but surrounded by cameras and microphones, Sonny whispered directly into Conrad's ear, "Any thoughts on, you know?"

"I'm getting closer." Conrad smiled, wanting to kiss Sonny.

"Babe." Sonny knotted his forehead and grabbed his own crotch, showing Conrad his need.

"Don't you even try to do that to me." Conrad laughed but his cock twitched in his shorts.

"Think about it. I was sure you'd come to my bed last night. I waited. Seriously, Conrad, I was surprised you didn't."

Conrad bit his lip and looked at the floor.

"You know, talking about moving to Philly. I can't say yes if you can't even make a tentative commitment here."

Instantly Conrad met his eyes. "Do not doubt my commitment to you."

"Yeah?" Sonny looked over his shoulder. "You and Tony are suddenly pals."

"Uh uh. Didn't happen. We both couldn't sleep and had a drink in the kitchen, talking."

"Am I supposed to believe that?"

"Yes."

"He's so hot for you."

"Takes two to horizontal bop." Conrad grew paranoid again, looking at the cameras. "He and I are holding out because we share the same problem. Families that will murder us."

Sonny gave Conrad a look of disbelief. "Yeah, that was my excuse."

"Sonny." Conrad reached for him as he walked away.

"He's here!" Kelvin bounced off the window and opened the front door.

The five men stood behind him as a long, black limousine parked in front. The chauffeur got out, opening the back passenger's door.

Conrad wondered if this man would live up to all the hype.

A tall, slender male with long flowing hair climbed out of the back. Dean caught Kelvin as he nearly fell over.

Watching this man strut, Conrad's gaze was drawn to his groin. The package he was seeing through skin-tight black slacks was beyond belief. Slowly raising his gaze to his face, Conrad's dick grew erect and he didn't even see the color of his eyes yet. "Green. Mother-fucker."

"Look at him," Alfonso moaned.

"Holy fucking shit!" Dean's gulp was audible.

"I'm gonna die." Sonny inhaled loudly.

"Hullo, lads." Mark extended his hand.

Kelvin stood like a zombie, his mouth open, his eyes wide.

Dean nudged him. "Say hello, Kelvin."

A squeak came out of Kelvin's throat.

"You have an ardent fan," Alfonso said, moving out of Mark's way as he entered the house.

"Do I?" Mark appeared amused. "Hullo, love." He touched Kelvin under his chin.

Conrad covered his laugh as Kelvin went completely mute and obviously star struck.

"I think he's goin' ta pass out," Tony said, laughing.

"All right, my pet. No need to act all silly." Mark held Kelvin's hand. "Which way?"

"That way." Sonny pointed to the back of the house.

"Why don't you show me, Kelvin?" Mark winked at Sonny.

While Kelvin managed to move his feet and lead Mark to the patio, the rest of the crowd watched.

"What a fucking ass!" Alfonso whimpered.

"Did you see the size of his dick?" Conrad asked.

Sonny replied, "You do realize you just said that out loud."

Conrad didn't and went red hot over his faux pas.

As if the men had just realized Mark was now outside, they clamored all over each other to get where he was, pushing and shoving their way to the back patio.

While Mark greeted the photographer with a kiss on the cheek, Kelvin swayed unsteadily.

"Come here, babycakes, before you fall over." Tony guided Kelvin to a lounge chair and they shared it.

Conrad really didn't expect this man to be as sensuous in person as his ads. It didn't make sense the photos weren't all doctored up to cover flaws and wrinkles. But hearing Mark, smelling him, and seeing him move, Conrad was so hard he was embarrassing himself.

A hand escorted Conrad to a chair. Conrad didn't take his eyes off of Mark as Sonny joined him on a lounge chair, much like the six of them had done while Keith and Carl were filming, but at least this time they could pant in lust and not get yelled at.

An assistant powdered Mark's face as Mark unbuttoned his top. Conrad heard Kelvin whimper.

Janis was occupied with her camera, as men tilted screens and backdrops to limit the shadows from the mid-day sun.

While someone took Mark's shirt, Mark's hair was brushed for him, fluffed up like a lion's mane.

"Oh, my fucking God." Conrad swallowed down a parched throat. Without thinking, he slid backwards, connecting to Sonny, who was behind him with his legs straddled around him. Sonny's thick cock throbbed against his ass. With Conrad's gaze connected to Mark's perfectly cut torso, Conrad reached for Sonny's hand and placed it on his own throbbing cock. "I'm out. I can't pretend this isn't putting me over the moon."

"That's my man." Sonny held him close, kissing his neck.

A fan was set up to blow back Mark's hair. As Mark postured for Janis, looking like walking sex, Kelvin hissed, "I'm going to cream."

Tony instantly reacted, embracing Kelvin from behind and cuddling him.

Though he didn't want to miss a thing Mark did, Conrad glanced over at Kelvin and Tony. Kelvin had both his hands down his own shorts as Tony rested his over the top of Kelvin's crotch.

"That's it, Mark," Janis said as her camera whirred and clicked. "Give me that fuck-me look."

Dean moaned in agony.

Conrad's dick throbbed and his shorts grew damp. "What is it about him?"

Sonny slid his hands towards Conrad's cock and gave it a squeeze. "Everything."

"Open your top button." Janis paused in her shooting.

Mark flipped open his trouser button, giving the housemates one of his most heated glances.

"*Ahh.*" Kelvin closed his eyes.

"Did he just come?" Sonny whispered into Conrad's ear.

"Yes. And if you keep squeezing my dick, so will I."

"One hand down the front." Janis crouched down, aiming her lens upwards.

Mark slid his right hand down his pants, licking his top lip.

"Fuck. Fuck." Conrad needed to stop the surge that was about to hit. He tried to dig inside his shorts to pinch it back, but Sonny wasn't having any of it. Instead, Sonny kept stimulating Conrad.

Seeing Mark's semi-erection through his unbelievably tight trousers, sans any underwear lines, meant one thing—commando. Conrad was mesmerized. "How the hell did a cop bag this guy?"

"Shut up and come."

Conrad realized Sonny was discreetly humping his ass at the same time as he was fondling him.

While Janis was kneeling, getting a camera filled with photos of this god, Mark stared at Conrad and tilted his head seductively, opening his zipper.

At a glimpse of dark pubic hair, Conrad came. His hips jerked into Sonny's moving hand and he closed his eyes and pressed his back hard against Sonny.

"Fuck," Sonny gasped into Conrad's ear.

Conrad felt Sonny's cock pulsating rapidly, obviously climaxing as well.

Blinking, Conrad caught Mark's knowing grin. Mark puckered and blew him a kiss.

"Son of a bitch." Conrad caught his breath and looked at Kelvin. Kelvin was panting so hard, Conrad expected him to pass out from hyperventilation.

With his fly half-way down, showing his glorious treasure trail and the top of his pubic bush, Mark combed his hands back through his mane and gave Janis an expression of orgasmic ecstasy.

Conrad heard both Dean and Alfonso grunt. Obviously everyone was shooting, not just Janis.

Janis stood straight, her attention on her camera. "Perfect. Thank you, Mark."

"No!" Kelvin yelled. "It's not over. More. Please."

Mark appeared bashful suddenly, as if he was only sexy for a camera. He closed his pant and was handed his shirt.

Tony said, "You might want to go wash your hands, Kelvin, in case Mark wants to shake it and say goodbye."

Kelvin took his fingers out of his shorts and pouted as he ran through the open sliding door.

"Is he bloody adorable or what?" Mark said as he finished buttoning his shirt.

"He's got one mean crush on you." Tony laughed.

"I'm flattered. Honest." Mark tucked his shirt in. "It was delicious. I enjoyed it."

Conrad hopped to his feet, petrified his stained shorts were now visible for the world to see. "It was really cool getting to meet you."

"My pleasure, I assure you." Mark shook their hands. "My assistant has a gift for each of you."

"Thank you, Mr. Richfield," Dean replied, his cheeks flushed.

"Oh, Mark, please," Mark waved at him, making a face of dismay. "I'm not mister to anyone."

Each of them were given a present of a black, silky box,

containing a bottle of cologne. Conrad gave it a sniff, then he leaned to have a snort from the source. “It smells better on you.”

Showing his perfect smile as he laughed, Mark replied, “Why does everyone say that?”

Kelvin emerged from the house.

Mark opened his arms. “Give us a hug, love.”

Racing for it, Kelvin latched onto Mark, hiding his face in Mark’s shirt.

“I am so honored, Kelvin, to have met you.”

“Mm!” Kelvin inhaled loudly. “I want you.”

Mark laughed sweetly. “Love, I am spoken for, otherwise, well, I may be tempted.”

“All right, babycakes.” Tony pried Kelvin off. “Let the busy man go.”

Conrad was deeply touched by Mark’s humility. Not an ounce of conceit was in him. And Mark had very good reason to be conceited.

Each housemate said goodbye as Mark was escorted out of the house, with his photographer right behind him.

“Bye, Janis, love.” Mark kissed her cheek. “Always a thrill.”

Conrad leaned against Sonny as they eavesdropped on the parting of friends in front of two waiting limousines.

“You too, Mark. You know I love seeing you.”

Mark waved at the men before he entered the back of the dark, stretch limo. When he vanished, Alfonso said, “Right. I’m a mess. Shower.” He held Dean’s hand and headed to the stairs.

Kelvin stood at the door until the cars drove off.

Assistants were still working on the patio to finish loading the equipment.

“Go wash up.” Tony patted Kelvin’s back.

Sonny glanced at Conrad. “Shower with me?”

“May as well.” Conrad took his hand. “I’m *out* all you sons of a bitches! Blame Mark Antonious Richfield!” Conrad roared into the house.

Will’s voice replied, “Congratulations, Conrad. Now you’re a real man.”

“Sure, Will.” Conrad laughed as he followed Sonny.

“Look at this!” Tony had opened the package Mark had given them. “A condom and lube as well as the cologne.”

“Really?” Sonny asked.

“Yeah.”

Conrad caught the gleam in Sonny’s eye as he continued to walk him to his room.

“I’m the top.” Conrad pointed to his chest.

“Sure you are.” Sonny nodded, obviously humoring him.

Kelvin yelled, “I love Mark Richfield.”

“Join the club.” Will laughed, his voice carrying throughout the house.

Conrad peeked back at Tony. To his surprise, he caught Tony with his arm around Kelvin, holding him close. “Looks like we’re all ‘real men’ now.”

“Huh?” Sonny asked.

“Nothing.”

Chapter Thirteen

Conrad passed his room to Sonny's bedroom. With fear trying to edge out the pleasure, Conrad figured he'd deal with the fallout later, after, some other time.

Not now. Not when he was so horny he could spurt…again.

Behind them two more bedroom doors shut. *Three couples. Unreal. Congratulations, Charlotte. You won.*

With the box of cologne in his hand, Sonny kept them moving to the bathroom. He closed the door, dug out the condom and lube and reached to place it inside the shower stall. Keeping his back to the camera, Sonny stripped off his shorts and briefs.

Conrad's body caught fire staring at him. Jet black hair grew from under Sonny's naval to his pubis, while Sonny's chest and low abdomen were shaved. Seeing Sonny's mocha colored erection had Conrad swooning as much as Mark Richfield had made Kelvin swoon.

Sonny yanked Conrad's clothing down, as if Conrad wasn't reacting quickly enough. Conrad's cock slapped his stomach when it was set free. Staring at Sonny made his length jerk in pulsating spasms.

Leaning into the shower, Sonny turned on the water, cupping his crotch to shield it from view as he held his hand under the water. Conrad got another good look at that barbed wire tattoo on Sonny's low back. He imagined fucking Sonny from behind, staring at it.

Once the shower warmed up, Sonny climbed in, dragging Conrad with him.

Sonny made sure the curtain was closed, end to end, and held Conrad as he backed under the spray, kissing him as they wet down.

Conrad moaned deeply, hearing it echo in the small space.

The feel of Sonny's mouth and his rough jaw against his made Conrad crazy. He gripped Sonny's face and deepened the kiss, sucking on his tongue while Sonny fucked Conrad's mouth with it.

While they kissed Conrad felt Sonny rubbing their cocks together, using his like a bat to slap against Conrad's thighs, balls, and his erection. Needing to pause for a breath, Conrad's head fell back and he moaned in yearning. Sonny chewed Conrad's throat, tugging on his balls and one of his nipples.

"Holy shit, Sonny." Conrad had never been handled like this. His ex was not romantic and only connected for the purpose of ejaculating. Sonny seemed to savor the foreplay.

It was at that moment that Conrad knew Sonny was top dog. While his genitals were being fondled and manipulated in a multitude of ways, Conrad received. He held Sonny's shoulders for balance and let this man do what he wished.

Sonny began his journey at Conrad's neck and licked his way to each nipple, spending time lapping at them, nibbling, rubbing his lips over them. While Sonny kissed down Conrad's torso, Conrad had to brace himself on the wall to not topple over.

Bypassing his cock, Sonny sucked on Conrad's balls, tugging them while they were inside his mouth. Conrad glanced down to see the pleasure on Sonny's face as water raced over his skin in glittering rivers.

When his cock was enveloped by Sonny's hot mouth, Conrad cried out from the pleasure and held Sonny's head. Matching movements, Conrad fucked Sonny's mouth as Sonny sucked hard and fast. Again his sack was massaged, along with the root of his dick and finally his rim. With one hand Sonny held the base of Conrad's cock, with the other, he pushed his finger inside Conrad's ass.

"Sonny! Augh!" Conrad's legs buckled. Wave after intoxicating wave of ecstasy rushed through Conrad's body. Seeing Sonny swallow as he milked him for every drop, Conrad was glad the shower was splashing his face because he was near tears he was so thrilled.

Sonny looked up at Conrad, smiling, as he used hard slow strokes to continue working Conrad's cock for every lingering wave of pleasure. The aftershocks were like nothing Conrad had ever felt.

Gently, Sonny coaxed Conrad to turn around.

Conrad couldn't catch his breath as he used the ledge of the tub to brace himself, and spread his legs. He knew it would hurt, but he wanted to give himself to Sonny.

Sonny used the lube to prepare Conrad. Conrad closed his eyes as he got a fabulous prostate massage. Glancing between his legs, he watched his cock spring up and down. Conrad pressed it between his legs, pointing it in Sonny's direction as a tease.

"Oh yeah…" Sonny laughed quietly.

The pressure of Sonny's cock on his ass made Conrad hold his breath.

"Relax," Sonny crooned, pushing in slowly.

Conrad cringed and tried to consciously release those constricted muscles.

"That's it." Sonny kept pushing in, deeper and deeper.

Conrad broke out in a cold chill even in the heat of the shower. "Fuck."

"Take a deep breath."

Obeying, Conrad inhaled, letting it out and forcing himself to unwind.

When Sonny held Conrad around his waist and rested his head on Conrad's back, Conrad whispered, "Are you all the way in?"

"Yes. Just relax."

Again Conrad inhaled deeply. The pain almost vanished.

"That's it, baby." Sonny seemed to know everything Conrad was feeling. He began pumping, gently, slowly.

"I'm okay." Conrad was determined to ride out the discomfort and feel the pleasure. After all, so many men loved to bottom.

His cock had gone soft from the apprehension, but now that the fear had vanished, Conrad began to enjoy giving Sonny his body this way. Hearing Sonny's pleasure was worth any sacrifice.

"Tell me I'm your first," Sonny purred as his thrusting grew in momentum.

"My first." Conrad closed his eyes. A spark of pleasure hit him.

"Tell me how much you love it."

The speed increased and Conrad's dick began to rise. "I…" Conrad gulped as the pain and pleasure morphed into something so rich he was speechless.

"Baby…baby…" Sonny thrust full throttle, holding Conrad's hips.

"Yes. Yes…come for me, come for me." Conrad felt Sonny's cock strongly pulsate. "Spurt in me."

Another deep thrust and Sonny's choking grunt echoed in the wet chamber. Conrad felt the rapid contractions deep inside his core. "Oh, God!" He loved it! Fucking loved it!

Sonny rested his head against Conrad's back, catching his

breath. Once Sonny was able to function, he pulled out and stood straight, closing his eyes and allowing the water to run down his face. Conrad turned around as Sonny removed the spent condom. "Look at you." Conrad shook his head. "You are gorgeous."

"I'm no Mark Richfield." Sonny laughed, tossing the rubber out of the shower and onto the toilet lid.

"No. But you're mine." Conrad embraced Sonny, kissing him.

Conrad couldn't deny taking a nap in Sonny's bed after hot sex was heaven. Snuggling, giggling, very close to sleeping soundly, Conrad felt like they were little kids doing something mischievous while their parents were away. He was light-headed from it.

Whatever the fallout, he'd deal with it later, after, some other time. Right now he had Sonny Washington in his arms. *Sorry, there's nothing better than this.*

Not realizing how long they had slept, Conrad woke, feeling drowsy and sated. He glanced at the digital clock. It was nearing six and that most likely meant Alfonso was making dinner. He smiled and pushed his nose into Sonny's neck, making kissing noises.

Sonny laughed; a low rumbling purr. "You're going to get me started."

Conrad grinned. "Yeah, but it'll be my turn to play top gun."

Sonny chuckled again, finally opening his eyes. They faced each other on the bed. Conrad felt the texture of Sonny's coarse jaw with the back of his hand.

"At least I'm not a virgin."

"Oh?" Conrad widened his eyes. Then it occurred to him. "Zack?" His smile fell.

"We weren't exclusive either way."

Conrad made a move to get out of bed.

"Whoa…hang on." Sonny held him back. "There's no reason to not talk about ex's is there? That's our history. We shouldn't have to hide it or be jealous."

"I don't have a letter tattooed on my dick."

Sonny let go his contact. "Are you really going to be like that?"

"No." Conrad rubbed his face and used the sheet to cover his groin from the camera. "I'm sorry."

"I'd have it removed but it would hurt like shit."

"It's okay. Honest."

Kelvin's voice came from outside the door. "You up, guys?"

"Yes." Conrad could tell Sonny was pissed at him.

"Alfonso said dinner's getting close."

"Okay, Kelvin." Conrad listened to Kelvin's footfalls fade. "I'm sorry, Sonny. I had a bad break up and I guess I'm still slightly raw."

"Am I your rebound?"

"No." Conrad hated that fucking camera. His luck, his ex would be watching, rubbing his hands greedily at still getting a mention on national TV. He'd be damned if he ever would speak his name. It was a name he'd sooner forget.

"What am I then?"

Conrad rested his chin in his palm. "My boyfriend? Can I be that lucky?"

"Yes. You can." Seeing Sonny smile was a relief. "But now we have to get dressed without flashing the world." Sonny shook his head.

"I'm beginning to resent that thing." Conrad tilted his head to the camera.

"Beginning to?" Sonny choked at the absurdity.

"One, two, three…" Conrad got out of bed, cupping his balls, racing to get to his room for fresh clothing. He could hear Sonny's laughter and joined it. It was funny, wasn't it?

The scent of baked food made Conrad's stomach grumble. He met Sonny in the hall and they held hands as they made their way to the kitchen.

"Well, well…" Alfonso smiled at their entrance. "They're out."

"Fuck it." Conrad shrugged. He glanced at Tony, mouthing, 'You?'

"I'm beginning to not give a shit. Had a shower with babycakes."

Sonny choked, coughing to hide his shock.

Kelvin smiled. "I think I know why they call him the Bronx Bomber."

"He's not a Yankee, Kelvin," Dean said, smiling.

"Still." Kelvin grinned, his eyes twinkling.

"I'm a Yankee fan. That's what counts." Tony headed to the fridge. "What are you boys drinking?"

"What's on offer?" Sonny sat on a stool at the island.

"Everything. Since we all pleased Ms. Deavers and Mr. Markham, it's become an open bar. And look at this." Tony tossed something from the counter at Sonny.

Sonny held a package of premium condoms.

"She sent a fucking load of them. With lube." Tony removed beer from the refrigerator and set a bottle before Sonny and Conrad.

"Son of a bitch." Sonny laughed. "That's it? Her work is done?"

Dean handed Sonny a bottle opener. "Oh, no. Not with two weeks left it isn't."

Conrad took the box from Sonny and inspected it. "Top of

the line. Spare no expense."

"What's for dinner, chef?" Sonny asked, sipping his beer.

"Lobster and crab lasagna with a béchamel sauce."

"Wow," Conrad said.

"Ya make the producers happy," Tony shrugged, "Ya get gold."

"Look at this!" Kelvin hopped over to a cabinet and opened it. "Barbeque flavored potato chips, and…chocolate truffles. Mm. My favorite." He waved the two items proudly.

Conrad stared at the camera directly. "Congratulations, Will. You won."

All the men paused, obviously waiting for a reply.

"What?" Tony threw up his hands. "Now he got what he wanted, he's gone?"

"Don't count on it." Dean shook his head.

Chapter Fourteen

After the evening meal, they relaxed by the pool.

Though none of the 'couples' were connected at the hip, Conrad wondered if for the rest of their stay things would be smooth sailing.

Kelvin splashed Tony playfully while Dean swam laps and Alfonso dozed on a lounge chair.

Sonny sat at the foot of Conrad's chaise, sharing a beer with him. "You sleeping in my bed tonight?"

"That's the plan," Conrad whispered, though secrecy was pointless now.

"Good." Sonny smoothed his hand along Conrad's shin.

The movement of the sliding door caught both Conrad and Sonny's attention. When a man wearing a white thong, bronzed, muscle-bound, blond with blue eyes, stunningly gorgeous, stepped out, Sonny gasped and Conrad sat upright like he was spring-loaded.

"Hello, gentlemen." The man's white teeth glowed from his tanned skin.

"Guys!" Conrad called to the others.

The playing in the pool ceased and Alfonso woke up.

"Who the fuck are you?" Tony asked in his usual eloquent manner.

"Your new housemate." He opened a bottle of baby oil and began rubbing it on his rounded pecs sensually.

"You have to be kidding me." Dean climbed out of the pool and grabbed a towel.

"Where you sleeping, goldilocks?" Tony asked, also getting out of the water.

"Why? Need a good fuck?" He grabbed his semi-erect dick and squeezed it. "I'm all bottom, honey."

"Holy shit," Alfonso said, "Is this a joke?"

"I'm Bruce. At your service." He massaged his cock with the oil which made it visible through the thin white fabric.

"Oh no," Kelvin moaned.

Conrad leaned close to Sonny's ear. "What? Are they testing us for loyalty now? Got us out, now let's see who cheats on their partner?"

"Huh?"

Conrad could see Sonny appeared smitten. He whacked him on the arm and Sonny woke up.

"Is it hot out?" Bruce slipped one hand inside his thong and stroked himself, rubbing his oiled nipples with his other hand.

Making the rounds visually to see everyone's reaction, Conrad thought it was like a dog park in August so many tongues were wagging.

"Blondie," Tony said, pointing to the camera, "Unless you want everyone to see if you're cut, point it the other way."

"Cut." He poked his dick out of his thong without any hesitation.

"Augh!" Kelvin sunk under the water but popped up soon after, continuing to stare.

"That'll be blurred out on TV," Alfonso said, "Poor viewing public. Missing the sight of that."

"Christ, how big is it?" Dean asked.

"Just a hair under nine, why?" Bruce exposed his entire cock, showing it off.

"Motha-fucka!" Sonny gawked.

Conrad hit him again to stop him. "Hey!"

Tony approached Bruce boldly. "So? What's the deal? I asked you where you're sleeping, new houseboy."

"Last unoccupied bedroom."

Conrad tried to think. "That locked door by the laundry?"

"It's not locked anymore, honey." Bruce pointed his cock at Conrad and Sonny, stroking with more zeal. "Open day or night, like my ass."

Kelvin moaned and dunked under the water again.

Tony shook his head. "Let me guess. Porn star."

"Go-go boy, porn star wanna be. Wanna be with me, stud?"

Looking straight in the camera Tony yelled, "What are you doin' to us, Will? Huh? We just got everything under control."

Alfonso laughed. "Tony, you just answered your own question."

"Tony?" Bruce sauntered closer. "I love that name."

"Don't you spray spunk on me." Tony backed up.

"Bet you fuck hard. Mmm, ahhh," Bruce made a face of pleasure. "Want to fight me and fuck me after? Huh? Mock rape?"

"Jesus H. Christ!" Tony appeared terrified.

Conrad had a good idea Bruce was given some secrets about them before he arrived. What was each of their weaknesses? Conrad didn't know Sonny's. He wasn't sure he knew his own.

"Put that thing away before you poke someone's eye out," Dean said, sitting with Alfonso.

Bruce aimed his cock at Dean, like a compass needle and

approached him. "Hmm, tattoo man. I know how you like it."

Dean went white as a sheet. "If you do, don't say it."

Bruce released his cock, crossed his wrists and stretched his hands over his head in a bondage pose. "Ahh, whip me, spank me."

Alfonso gaped at Dean. "Yeah? Is he right?"

"No!" Dean replied but looked horrified.

Sonny chuckled.

Conrad watched the wild-man take notice of Sonny because of his laugh. Bruce stalked Sonny and Sonny shrunk back against Conrad from fear.

"Mm, dark meat." Bruce licked his lips. "My favorite. I'd rim you for an hour, sugar."

Conrad both heard and felt Sonny clear his throat as he pressed against him.

"Pure bottom…" Bruce jerked his cock a few times. "I'd never ask you to bottom, alpha dog."

"Shut the fuck up!" Conrad felt defensive.

"And you?" Bruce closed in on Conrad as Sonny cringed and tried to get away from the aim of that mighty nearly nine-incher. "What's your fantasy, construction man? Work boots and white socks? A tool belt? Big tools?"

Conrad hid his face from the camera. Just what his father and brothers needed to hear, he got off on the other guys on the job.

"You're scary!" Kelvin pointed at him.

Bruce dove into the water, tossing his tiny g-string onto the ledge. He swam to a petrified looking Kelvin, while Tony bristled.

"I'd be so gentle with you, baby." Bruce picked Kelvin up under water and physically wrapped each of Kelvin's legs around his waist. "Bet the Italian stud doesn't want you to top. I'd love it."

"Oh…" Kelvin melted.

"All right," Tony said. "Break it up before I get violent."

"I don't mind if you two share me." Bruce gave Tony an imploring look. "I'll take it at both ends."

Conrad was dying. "What are you doing to us, Charlotte?" he shouted.

"Torture." Alfonso shook his head.

Bruce released Kelvin and waded to the ladder. When he climbed out, water running down his oily, naked body, Conrad knew everyone's cock was throbbing and seeping at the sight.

He walked towards Alfonso, his dick protruding from his groin like a mast, directed at Alfonso's mouth. "Want everyone to know what you like, chef?"

"No." Alfonso went beet red.

"Pretty please? With whipped cream and a cherry on the top?" Bruce pouted out his bottom lip, wagging his rod at him.

Dean spun on the chair to look at Alfonso. "Whipped cream? With all your low fat recipes you do it with whipped cream?"

"And chocolate sauce. Mm!" Bruce thrust his cock at Alfonso.

Conrad imagined Alfonso opening his mouth to receive it. Instead, Alfonso turned away in embarrassment.

Kelvin climbed out of the water nervously. Tony wrapped a towel around his shoulders, drying him.

Bruce stood back, making sure he gave each housemate a good sultry stare. When he met Conrad's eye, Conrad felt the breath catch in his throat. *This is so not good. None of us have a strong relationship. We've known each other a week.*

Bruce reclined in a lounge chair and held out the oil. "Anyone want to rub my body? Anywhere they'd like?"

A chorus of 'No!' followed.

Laughing, Bruce raised the bottle and dribbled the oil

down his chest, massaging his flawless physique.

"Come on, babycakes." Tony held Kelvin's hand. "We don't need to watch the showoff." While Tony dragged Kelvin into the house, Kelvin was riveted to Bruce's actions until he had gone inside.

Conrad tore his gaze away from Bruce, only to see Sonny gawking at him.

Bruce's body glistening naked in the sun was obviously either too much for the housemates to handle, or too much to not to handle.

Catching Sonny trying to ogle without being seen got on Conrad's nerves. "I'm going in. Are you?"

"Huh?" Sonny snapped out of his apparent daydream.

"Never mind." Conrad climbed off the lounge chair.

"No. I'm coming." Sonny tripped as he followed, his head aiming in the wrong direction for his feet.

The minute he and Sonny were inside, Conrad gripped Sonny's shoulder and dragged him to the lounge. "I know we're not a real couple yet."

"Wait. Wait a minute…" Sonny shook his head and held up his hands as if he knew what Conrad was going to say.

"But ya want to see flesh, Sonny? Huh?" Conrad tore his t-shirt off and yanked down his shorts and briefs, kicking them off.

"Conrad!" Sonny tried to hide the camera's view of his crotch. "What are you doing, man?"

Conrad held out his arms. "Do I compare? Huh? Do I? Or is Bruce-the-ho more enticing?"

"Jesus! You do realize you're on camera." Sonny grabbed Conrad's shorts and held them over his dick.

"You want me to rim you for an hour? Fine. You want to play top dog? Okay."

"Calm down."

"Anything. Just tell me you will not touch that asshole!"

"Put your clothes on, Conrad." Sonny tried to hand him his shorts and briefs.

"Sonny!" Conrad's voice broke.

"Wow!" Kelvin stopped short. "Conrad…what a bod. Ah, you know this is on TV right?"

Tony appeared behind Kelvin. "Son of a bitch! Conrad…you fantastic fucker." Tony called out, "Alfonso, Dean, you gotta come and see this one."

Conrad glared into Sonny's eyes in a stalemate. Sonny kept Conrad's shorts in front of his groin but they didn't say a word.

"Wow. Babe." Dean whistled. He walked behind Conrad for the view. "A tat. Right there."

Conrad felt Dean's finger press on his ass cheek.

"Am I missing something?" Bruce poked his head around the wall.

"Get lost." Alfonso nudged him. "We found someone prettier than you. Scram."

"What?" Bruce laughed nervously.

Sonny asked, "You putting your clothing on?"

Conrad replied, "You fucking that slut?"

"Hell no."

"No one is." Alfonso pushed Bruce backwards, away from the lounge.

"No one?" Kelvin asked quietly.

"Go for it, babycakes." Tony grinned. "You fuck him, I'll stick my dick in his mouth."

"No kidding?" Kelvin draped his arms around Tony's neck and embraced him. "You'd let me do that?"

"Yeah. You ain't toppin' me, so you may as well do someone willing."

Conrad took his shorts from Sonny and put them on.

"Show's over." Dean waved for everyone to clear out.

Trying not to be furious, Conrad held his briefs and shirt, passing everyone in the hall, including Bruce as he headed to the stairs. "Nice try, asshole."

"Don't blame me." Bruce grinned.

Conrad glared at a camera as he walked. "I know who to blame."

Walking up the stairs, Conrad noticed an excited Kelvin holding both Tony and Bruce's hands as he scampered into Bruce's bedroom.

"Whatever," Conrad breathed, closing the door to his room behind him. He threw his clothing on his bed and was about to pick up his diary cam to give his thoughts to it when his door opened.

Sonny closed it behind him and sat on the bed. "Go on. I want to hear what you tell it."

"It's personal."

Smiling, Sonny said, "You think it's not broadcast live?"

"Yeah, but you won't hear it."

"Sit." Sonny patted the bed.

Walking around to the opposite side, Conrad reclined on the pillows. Sonny mirrored his posture. "I want you. We discussed you relocating to Philly. We came out against our will for each other."

Conrad's stomach tightened. Was this a kiss off or a kiss 'on'?

"Are you the possessive-jealous type, Conrad? Or do you have trust in people?"

"I'm the jealous type. My ex made sure I knew he was not monogamous and didn't lie about it nor hide his conquests."

"What did you see in him?"

"Good question."

"Sex?"

"At first. But it doesn't compare to what we do."

Sonny scooted closer so they were touching from the waist down. "When I go back to med school, I'll be one hundred percent swamped with studies. But…I won't cheat on you if we establish ourselves as a couple."

"Okay." Conrad was relieved.

"I won't have a lot of downtime. I'll be at school, studying, labs…you have any idea what that will be like?"

"No. Not a clue."

"You'll think I'm neglecting you. But I won't be. I'll be working for our future."

Conrad blinked. "Our future?"

A confused expression passed over Sonny. "Man, how am I getting this all wrong?"

"No!" Conrad dove on him and spread his legs around Sonny's. "I'm just amazed a guy with so much going for him wants an unemployed construction worker."

"Is that all you are?"

Dean's voice yelled from the lower floor, "Come on, guys! Not everyone has to hear your three-way fuck session!"

Cringing, Conrad tried not to imagine the moaning coming from Bruce's room.

"Glad we're up here." Sonny laughed.

"Me too." Conrad pinned Sonny to the bed and kissed him. He heard Sonny moan and felt him open his mouth wider.

Conrad rode his hard dick over Sonny's, igniting the flame in both of them. "I'm top," Conrad breathed between kisses.

Sonny laughed seductively.

"Get under the blanket before I show the universe just whose lover you are." Conrad pecked Sonny's lips and rolled off of him, searching in the nightstand drawer into the ridiculously large supply of lubrication and condoms.

They used the blankets as a tent and hid under it. With a few quick movements, they were naked and grinding again under cover. Trying not to shriek in pleasure like the trio in Bruce's bedroom, Conrad focused on Sonny's mouth, his swirling techniques and the way he licked his cock the same way as he was manipulating his tongue. "If I don't get in you, I'll come." Conrad dry humped Sonny's pelvis, feeling both their cocks becoming sticky.

"Okay, alpha dog." Sonny rolled to his stomach, raising his hips off the bed.

"Oh, yes, oh, yes." Conrad grew hotter than ever at the sight of that tattoo, getting to stare at it as he fucked. He pinched his dick to slow down and fussed to keep the sheets on the bed.

Shaking, Conrad opened the condom and stared at Sonny's tat as he unrolled it onto his dick. Before he lubed them both up, he licked Sonny's ass. "Like rimming?"

Sonny groaned in ecstasy.

Conrad gripped an ass cheek in each hand, spread wide and went for him. Hearing Sonny grunt and groan almost made Conrad climax. After chewing on each tight globe of Sonny's perfect ass, he shot lubrication directly into his hole.

"Fuck! It's cold."

"All right, hot stuff. It'll warm up in that cauldron of heat you've become." Conrad chuckled. Pointing his cock at his puckered rim, Conrad began to slide in. "Tell me if you want me to stop."

Hearing Sonny inhale and exhale deeply, Conrad waited, trying to be patient like Sonny had been with him.

But in one swift movement, Sonny jammed his hips backwards, making Conrad's cock enter to the hilt.

"Aghh!" Conrad gasped. "What the fuck?"

"Shut up and screw me, gorgeous."

"You son of a bitch!" Conrad began hammering into him

happily. "You will be my bottom boy."

"You will be mine."

Conrad licked Sonny's back, enjoying his salty sweat. "You got that right." He thrust in deeper and faster. "I am so there."

"Jack me off."

Fumbling to get to Sonny's cock, Conrad felt how thick and hard Sonny had gotten from the internal massage. He gripped his stiff length and pulled it in time with his manic thrusting.

"Yeah, yeah…" Sonny matched the rhythm.

"Babe…oh, babe…" Conrad couldn't hold out. He grunted and swallowed his scream, feeling his groin contract and tense up as his dick throbbed like his racing pulse.

Cream coated Conrad's fingers and Sonny's entire body went rigid under him. Conrad used the spunk to jack hard and slow on Sonny, milking and prolonging his climax as he kept pumping his hips, enjoying his own aftershocks.

Sonny collapsed under him and Conrad landed heavily on top.

"Got to get Kelvin to do the laundry." Sonny moaned.

For some reason Conrad thought that was hilarious. He began laughing in an uncontrollable fit as Sonny obviously found it contagious. They laughed until they had exhausted themselves, lying still, sticky and satisfied.

Chapter Fifteen

Perhaps because his seduction had fallen flat, Bruce didn't stay the night.

Over dinner, Kelvin boasted about his first chance to top another man, as Tony smiled like a proud papa at him.

Conrad allowed the dinner to digest as the housemates laughed together and drank their fill of beer and wine, still seated at the dining room table.

Suddenly Will's voice sounded over the invisible speakers. "Congratulations, men. Enjoy the rest of your stay."

Dean asked, "You done torturing and testing us?"

"I am."

Six fists met in the middle of the table to rejoice.

Will said, "Just be prepared for the outside world. Savor your surreal utopia while you can."

Sonny met Conrad's eyes. All the men's joy suddenly evaporated to anxiety.

"Fucking party pooper!" Alfonso said in anger.

"Took the fucking words outta my mouth." Tony sneered.

"Though they call this 'reality' TV," Will said, "We know better than that, don't we?"

Kelvin shivered visibly. "I don't want to go back home. I hate to admit, I like it like this."

Tony caressed Kelvin's hair. "You'll be okay, babycakes."

"What about you, Tony?" Conrad asked, "How will you be?"

"Moving!" he laughed but his humor didn't convince anyone.

"First thing I'm doing when I get out," Dean said, "Is contacting all the tattoo joints in the O.C."

Alfonso reached to him for a kiss.

"What about you, Conrad?" Kelvin asked.

"Heading to Philly." Conrad took a sheepish glance at the camera as if it were his father's admonishing eye.

"I'm so happy for you guys." Dean reached his hand to Sonny and Conrad.

"He hasn't experienced how hard it's going to be while I'm in med school." Sonny pointed his thumb at Conrad.

"You want me there?" Conrad asked.

"Yes!" Sonny answered loudly.

"Then shut up." Conrad winked at him.

Chapter Sixteen

Without anymore interference, and getting every item or wish they had requested, the rest of the time inside their private haven was bliss. Other than good natured fun teasing, no one battled, three couples slept together every night, and because everyone was eternally sexually satisfied, life became a routine of exercise, great cuisine, fabulous conversations, and a bond that had grown into love.

But…

The last day had arrived.

Will's voice advised them of the hour they needed to clear out, and Charlotte sent helpers to get them packed up.

A pile of luggage sat waiting in the hall.

Conrad knew how he felt about leaving this group, and his emotions were reflected in five men.

Kelvin kept dabbing at the corner of his eye but didn't voice his pain.

When one of the men who assisted in their packing set a stack of notepads and pens on the kitchen counter, Alfonso said, "Thank fuck. About time." He raced towards them, handing one to each housemate. "Let's go. Whole names, addresses, cell phone, email…"

Conrad took the paperwork anxiously and sat in the lounge.

Sonny suggested, "Write it on one, pass the paper and we'll each put our info down."

"My genius," Conrad said as Sonny sat next to him. In gratitude, Sonny kissed Conrad on the lips.

Busy passing pages around, Conrad heard the door and glanced up. Charlotte was there. "Time to go, boys."

Sickness overwhelmed Conrad and he felt his stomach knot.

"Tony, Kelvin, Dean, and Sonny, you get in the first limo. It's going to the airport. Conrad, you're in limo number two, headed to Northern Cal, and Alfonso, you're in limo three, headed to So-Cal. Got it?"

Conrad felt his eyes burn with tears and looked at Sonny.

"Don't worry." Sonny gripped Conrad's knee.

Conrad leapt towards Sonny, embracing him and kissing him as hot tears ran down his cheeks.

"It's okay. I'll be there." Sonny held him tight. "Just get your shit together and come out."

Conrad nodded when words failed him.

Standing, Sonny hauled Conrad to his feet and gave him his piece of paper with all of their names on it. "I'll call you the minute I get a chance."

"Yes." Conrad used the back of his hand to wipe his eyes. When he looked up Conrad saw five men all gazing at each other in agony.

"Babe." Alfonso reached out to Conrad, his eyes flooded with tears.

They met in a circle in the middle of the lounge, holding each other. Conrad kissed each of them, tasting salty tears on his lips.

"Guys, we'll visit," Dean whispered. "We made a connection here."

"Tony." Conrad held him around the waist. "Don't go

through it alone. We're all here."

"I love you guys." Tony tried to smile. "I'll be okay, Conrad."

Kelvin began sobbing.

"Shh, babycakes. I'll be with you in the limo." Tony comforted him.

"Guys?" Charlotte tapped her shoe.

One by one they met for the last goodbye. Conrad held each man by the jaw and kissed his lips. Standing before Sonny he stared into his eyes and bit his lip.

Sonny seemed speechless suddenly and nodded.

Conrad mouthed, 'Love you.'

'You too.' Sonny's eyes overflowed and he wiped them roughly.

Charlotte opened the front door. The moment Conrad was able to see outside, he realized the fence had been removed. He gasped at an enormous crowd of spectators, squealing and waving at them from behind security, the limousines, and a camera crew.

Some fans carried signs with hearts and their names on it, like *Dean and Alfonso forever*, or *Sonny and Conrad, true love*. One sign said, *We love you, Tony. Be strong*. Another said, *We vote Kelvin the most adorable*.

"What the hell is this?" Tony walked slowly to the first limo.

"Your fans." Charlotte waved her arm grandly.

Seeing nearly two hundred people, hearing their deafening roar of approval, Conrad knew the welcome home party in Elk Grove would not be as supportive. He felt for Tony. Tony had it bad when he got back to New York.

Though the noise was a distraction, Conrad looked one last time at Sonny. They met eyes and Sonny smiled.

Conrad threw him a kiss. Sonny caught it and put it into his pocket.

Giving the housemates who weren't too overwhelmed by the noisy exit a nod or wave, Conrad stood back as the chauffeur opened the door for him. Once he climbed in, he closed his eyes and rested his head on the back seat, ignoring the roar of voices from outside.

Reality? His reality had just begun.

Dozing on and off on the drive from the house to his own apartment, Conrad woke to hear the back door opening. He shook his head to clear it and rubbed his eyes.

The man in black set his luggage on the pavement in front of his apartment house. "Do you need help getting it inside?"

"No. Thanks." Conrad shook his hand.

"Good luck to you, sir."

"I'll need it," Conrad muttered as he hoisted his bag and backpack and made for the front lobby door.

The first thing he did after dropping his things into his bedroom was look at his message machine. The light was blinking.

Five messages were waiting.

Before he listened to them, he stopped at the bathroom to freshen up, then took a bottle of vodka out of his kitchen cabinet, and drank a shot. "Okay. Here we go."

He stood at the nightstand and pushed, play on his recording machine.

"What the fuck?" his brother Hank asked, "You're a fucking homo?"

Hitting delete, Conrad cringed as he waited for the next one. His second brother, Ashley, had similar thoughts. "You fuckhead! What the hell's wrong with you? You know what that shit did to dad?"

Delete.

"Mother-fucker, Conrad? You been queer all this time? Staring at the guys on the construction site? I'm sick to my stomach." Hearing a co-worker taking the same low moral ground made Conrad ill.

"Fuck you, Bo." Conrad hit delete and was becoming numb.

Another friend, Arnie was next in line to spit in Conrad's face. "Fuck. You idiot. I can't believe I went out for a beer with you. Were you leering at my ass? You make me sick."

As if he couldn't help himself, he listened to the final one. Hearing his ex-boyfriend, John's voice was the last thing Conrad needed or expected. "Man, I knew you were stupid, but outting yourself on that pathetic show was even more moronic than you normally are. Glad you and I aren't together anymore. Good luck!"

Delete.

Conrad dropped to the bed and hunched over, hiding his face in his hands. "Thanks, Charlotte. Thanks a lot."

He napped but didn't know for how long he had.

The phone rang and it startled him. Thinking of the terrible messages, Conrad became hesitant to pick it up. His machine did for him. He heard Sonny's voice and grabbed it. "Hey."

"Hey. Screening calls?"

"Yeah." Conrad scratched his head and jaw.

"Uh oh."

"You don't even want to know the messages I had on my machine."

"From who?"

"My two brothers, a couple of friends and my ex, believe it or not."

"Your ex? He want you back now?"

"No. He thinks I'm a dumbshit and he's glad he and I

aren't together. I even make that asshole sick."

"Baby." Sonny sounded tired. "Fly out. I miss you."

Conrad looked around his apartment. "Can I?'

"Can you?" Sonny laughed softly.

"I mean like tomorrow?"

"Yes!"

A spark of hope kindled in Conrad. "You sure you mean it, because I will."

"Uh hum? Conrad Hogan. I mean it."

He smiled and felt shy. "I love you."

"Then get your tight ass on a plane and come here."

"As soon as I pack."

"Let me know your flight time. I'll pick you up."

The relief Conrad felt was immense. "I'll get on line now and book tickets."

"Can't wait. Miss you, Conrad. You have no idea how much."

Conrad cupped the phone as if it were Sonny's cheek. "You too. Baby, I'll be good to you. I'll treat you like gold."

"I know you will, lover."

"I'll email you the confirmation when I get it."

"See you soon."

"Thank you, Sonny."

"Thank me? Are you kidding me?" Sonny chuckled.

The emotion Conrad felt, the connection, was like nothing he had before in his life. "I'm on my way."

"That's what I need to hear. Love you. See you soon."

"You too." Conrad hung up and just before he stood to go to the computer, he sat back down and unfolded the piece of paper he had in his hand. Picking up the phone, he dialed. A machine answered. "Tony, it's Conrad…"

Immediately Tony picked up. "Hey."

"Hey, babe." Conrad said, "Was it horrible?"

"I'm packing. I got to get my ass out of here." Tony sounded scared.

"Me too. I'm flying out to Philly first thing tomorrow."

"I'm headed to Rain City."

"Yeah? To hang out with Kelvin?"

"The boy needs a teacher, ya know what I mean?"

"Oh, sweetheart. You pretend to be a tough guy, but you're sweet as sugar."

"Don't you dare spill that or I'll put you in a lead bathing suit."

"Look. Are you going to be okay?" Conrad was afraid for him.

"I will be. I just stopped home for some shit I needed to do. I booked a flight to Seattle while I was still in Newark airport."

"Call me at Sonny's."

"I will, babe. We knew it would be like this for us."

"I was hoping for the best but I got the worst."

"I knew I'd get the worst, so I was a step ahead of you."

Conrad paused to listen to Tony's breathing. "You know I love you."

"I love you too, Conny. Us six. We won't lose touch."

"No. Maybe we'll all meet in LA."

"Perfect. Let me go before some goon comes to my door and executes me."

"Shit. Tony!"

"I'm teasin'. Let me go."

"Call me!" Conrad was terrified for him.

"I will. Don't you worry. No one's going to hurt me."

"Okay. See ya."

"See ya."

Conrad disconnected the line, took a minute to digest the news, then hopped to his feet to pack and make flight arrangements. He'd deal with the rest long distance. If his family thought he was an outcast now? Fine. He was done with them.

Turning on the computer, Conrad booked the flight to Philadelphia, yearning his man.

Afterword

The noise of music and the laughter of men made it hard to talk and be heard. Conrad admired a sleek go-go boy in a suspended cage as he gyrated his hips, showing off his big package.

Warmth pressed up behind him. Conrad looked over his shoulder at Sonny's smile. "Are you mesmerized?"

Conrad laughed softly. "You went to get a drink. I had to do something to distract me."

"Come on. The boys are over there."

Conrad held Sonny's waist as they maneuvered between men to a group laughing and drinking in the flashing strobe lights.

Kelvin was topless, waving his shirt like a banner over his head, dancing.

"Looks like LA agrees with the Seattleite." Conrad gestured to Kelvin.

"Dontcha just love him?" Tony snuggled behind Kelvin and licked his neck.

"We know someone who does." Alfonso winked at Dean.

"So? When are you coming in for your tat, Conrad?" Dean nudged him.

"When can you do it?"

"Tomorrow?"

"Deal." Conrad grinned at Sonny.

Dean told Sonny, "He's getting a blazing sun on his low back, babe. Gee, I wonder why?"

Conrad hooked his elbow around Sonny's neck and kissed him. "Wish he could erase that Z from his dick."

"Want me to make it into something else, Sonny?" Dean asked.

"We'll work on it." Sonny smiled.

"I can get used to this." Kelvin rested his back against Tony's chest. "You know, all six of us together again."

"Come live in LA." Alfonso gestured to the abundance of gay men.

"After med school. Maybe." Sonny tilted his head.

"Yeah?" Conrad couldn't stop touching him.

"Yeah." Sonny set his drink aside and grabbed Conrad's waist, rubbing dicks as they danced.

Conrad still had to make peace with his family, but he had time. He was living with Sonny and had found a construction job. There wasn't anything more he needed.

Gripping Sonny close as they danced, Conrad looked over his shoulder at his best friends. They were laughing and enjoying the reunion immensely.

"Hey!" Conrad called to them. They all perked up. "Any of you got men?"

"We all do, hotstuff," Tony replied, roughhousing with Kelvin.

"Out!" Dean hollered in triumph. "Out and loving it!"

Alfonso picked Dean off his feet to spin him around.

Sonny roared with laughter at their antics. He met Conrad's gaze and said, "Not all bad came out of that madness."

“No. Not all bad. I found the love of my life.”

“Sweet talker you.” Sonny batted his lashes.

“Give me a kiss, handsome.”

Sonny dipped Conrad and met his lips.

There was only one reality for Conrad. Sonny. That was all he needed.

The End

About the Author

Award-winning author G. A. Hauser was born in Fair Lawn, New Jersey, USA, and attended university in New York City. She moved to Seattle, Washington where she worked as a patrol officer with the Seattle Polic Department. In early 2000 G.A. moved to Hertfordshire, England, where she began her writing in earnest and published her first book, *In the Shadow of Alexander*. Now a full-time writer in Ohio, G.A. has written dozens of novels, including several bestsellers of gay fiction. For more information on other books by G.A., visit the author at her official website at: www.authorgahauser.com.

G.A. has won awards from All Romance eBooks for Best Novel 2007, *Secrets and Misdemeanors*, Best Author 2007. Best Novel 2008, *Mile High*, and Best Author 2008.

The G.A. Hauser Collection

Available Now

Single Titles

Unnecessary Roughness

Got Men?

Heart of Steele

All Man

Julian

Black Leather Phoenix

In the Dark and What Should Never Be, Erotic Short Stories

Mark and Sharon (formerly titled A Question of Sex)

A Man's Best Friend

It Takes a Man

The Physician and the Actor

For Love and Money

The Kiss

Naked Dragon

Secrets and Misdemeanors

Capital Games

Giving Up the Ghost

To Have and To Hostage

Love you, Loveday

The Boy Next Door

When Adam Met Jack

Exposure

The Vampire and the Man-eater

Murphy's Hero

Mark Antonious deMontford

Prince of Servitude

Calling Dr. Love

The Rape of St. Peter

The Wedding Planner

Going Deep

Double Trouble

Pirates

Miller's Tale

Vampire Nights

Teacher's Pet

In the Shadow of Alexander

The Rise and Fall of the Sacred Band of Thebes

The Action Series

Acting Naughty

Playing Dirty

Getting it in the End

Behaving Badly

Dripping Hot

Packing Heat

Men in Motion Series

Mile High

Cruising

Driving Hard

Leather Boys

Heroes Series

Man to Man

Two In Two Out

Top Men

G.A. Hauser
Writing as Amanda Winters

Sister Moonshine

Nothing Like Romance

Silent Reign

Butterfly Suicide

Mutley's Crew

Made in the USA
Middletown, DE
27 April 2015